I0653606

HEXES
and
HEDGEHOGS

Familiar Spirits · Book 3

CHRISTINE POPE

Dark Valentine Press

HEXES AND HEDGEHOGS

Copyright © 2023 by Christine Pope

ISBN: 978-1-946435-68-2

Published by Dark Valentine Press

Cover design by Danielle Fine

Ebook formatting by Indie Author Services

Chapter 1

Dating Game

I blinked at Detective Derek Falco, who was standing a few feet away from me near the counter in my apothecary shop, his expression pleasant, if a little puzzled. Most likely, he'd never had a woman hesitate this long in response to an invitation to dinner. Maybe four or five years older than my own twenty-nine, he was a little more than six feet tall, with sooty black hair and equally dark eyes, and the sort of classically handsome features you might see on a statue in a villa in Rome.

But he still was no match for Noah Jenkins, the veterinarian and all-around amazing person I'd started dating recently.

Knowing I needed to say something before the strained silence grew any more awful, I blurted, "I'm seeing someone."

Derek might have blinked, although overall, his expression didn't change upon hearing my announcement. "Oh," he said, sounding fairly unruffled. "I'm sorry. I kind of heard through the grapevine that you were single."

Had he been making inquiries about me? I supposed that wasn't so strange, considering the first time we'd met was when I'd come to him a few days earlier with damning recorded evidence from a woman named Lorna Miller, who'd implicated her husband Thad in the murder of their son. It only made sense that Derek would have wanted to check into my background, just to make sure I was legit and wasn't harboring some kind of secret grudge against the Millers.

That definitely wasn't the case, since I'd only met them a few weeks earlier, after Noah's ex-fiancée Shelby had found their son Trevor dead on the floor of her rented Airbnb.

Or maybe it was more that Derek had decided I was cute and wanted to make sure he wasn't stepping on any toes.

There were definitely toes to be stepped on, though. I couldn't say that whatever was going on between Noah Jenkins and me was precisely formal, even if I did tend to think of him as my boyfriend. I'd never referred to him that way in public, though, and probably wouldn't until I heard him call me his girlfriend first.

I was just cautious that way.

To my relief, I summoned what I hoped was a friendly but not at all provocative smile. "Well, Noah and I have only been seeing each other for a couple of weeks, but I'm still in a place where I'm not really interested in dating anyone else."

For the first time, Derek Falco's own smile slipped a little. "Noah Jenkins?"

"Yes," I replied, even as I wondered how Derek knew about Noah. Was my new almost-boyfriend a speed demon or something, someone who'd gotten pulled over by the cops more than once? After all, Salem was a big enough town, with more than 45,000 residents, that it wasn't as though everyone who lived there could possibly know everyone else. I'd never noticed Noah speeding whenever he drove, but I supposed he could have been trying to hold back for my sake.

"He provides vet services for our K-9 units," Derek offered, and I relaxed a little. I hadn't even considered that Noah might give some kind of professional help to the local authorities. Salem's police force wasn't huge, but I knew they had a couple of dogs who served alongside the officers, mostly for sniffing out drugs, that kind of thing. And even though Salem had several vet clinics, Noah's was the one located closest to the police station, making it that much more convenient.

"Oh, that's nice," I said, knowing even as I

spoke how inane those words must have sounded. Then again, maybe that was a good thing. If Derek decided I was an utter airhead, he probably wouldn't have any desire to keep pressing his suit.

"Yes, Noah's a good guy," Derek responded. It was entirely possible he'd already realized that going out with me was a lost cause, so there wasn't any reason not to praise his rival.

Or he could just be a decent guy who doesn't have a problem with complimenting people who deserve it, I told myself, my mental tone a little sharp. *Not everything has to be a competition.*

"Well," Derek continued, "I won't take up any more of your time. Have a good one."

He inclined his head toward me, then turned and headed out the door. A pause as he held it open for Sage Halloran, my assistant, who'd chosen that precise moment to return. She had a bag of sandwiches in one hand and a tray with two cups of iced tea in the other, and looked utterly grateful for the help.

After Derek was gone and the door had shut behind him, Sage sent me an inquiring look. "Who was that?"

"Derek Falco," I said, and added, "He's a detective with the Salem P.D. He just wanted to drop in and thank me for helping with the Miller case."

It seemed my explanation made enough sense

to her that she didn't ask any other...possibly prob-ing...questions. "Oh, that was nice of him," she replied as she set the bag of sandwiches and the tray of teas on the counter next to the cash register. "Do you want me to cover for you while you eat?"

That was usually how we handled our midday meal at the store—one of us would watch the cash register and generally keep an eye on things while the other person went into the break room to have her lunch. Today, though, I wasn't really that hungry, even though it was now almost one-thirty.

"You go ahead," I told Sage, hoping my appetite would return by the time she was done. "I can wait."

She gave me a grateful smile, and took the bag of sandwiches and one of the iced teas with her into the back room where I had a small table, a dorm-size refrigerator, and a tiny microwave. After she was gone, I reached for my iced tea and helped myself to a sip. Maybe caffeine wasn't really supposed to soothe your nerves, but I still felt a little better anyhow.

But even though Noah and I had known each other casually for more than a year—he'd bought a vet practice here in Salem right around then—it wasn't until I'd enlisted his help in finding Milo, the cocker spaniel familiar I'd been fostering, that things started to heat up between the two of us.

Milo was now a permanent fixture in my household, since his mistress Darla Fitzgerald had been murdered, and I couldn't imagine the dog going to live with anyone else. Naturally, Noah didn't think of Milo as anything more than an extremely friendly, intelligent example of his breed, and I needed to keep things that way for the foreseeable future.

As a witch—a Salem witch, to boot—I had to make absolutely sure things were rock solid between Noah and me before I could allow myself to confide in him. Right now, he only knew me as the owner of Full Moon Apothecary, located on one of Salem's most touristy streets, and nothing more.

All right, maybe a little bit more than that. Only a few days earlier, we'd been intimate for the first time, and I knew our relationship had irrevocably changed. In a good way, of course, but still, even though I knew I'd never met anyone like Noah Jenkins before, and even though I hoped this was only the start of bigger and better things, I realized I had to be careful.

And being careful meant I needed to stay far, far away from Derek Falco. Even if I were just as single as he'd believed me to be, I knew getting involved with someone on the local police force would open a whole extra-messy can of worms. In general, the witch community did its best to avoid any contact with the authorities, simply because we couldn't afford for them to learn anything about the magical world that bubbled along just under the surface of regular people's everyday lives. Maybe the argument could be made that if Derek was really "the one," he'd know he needed to protect the woman he loved and make sure no one else on the force ever learned there was anything particularly unusual about her...or her family and friends.

But since Derek really didn't have a chance, thanks to Noah's presence in my life, at least I didn't have to worry about that extra bit of complication.

Should I tell Noah that Derek had asked me out?

On the surface, the thought seemed kind of ridiculous. Yes, Noah and I were involved in each other's lives now, but we definitely hadn't progressed to the point where we thought it necessary to tell each other absolutely everything. And what would be the point, anyway? To make him jealous? To let him know there were other men who were interested in me, just in case things didn't work out between the two of us?

That notion was even more ridiculous.

I sipped some more tea and was glad to be

temporarily distracted by the arrival of a large group of tourists who'd just stepped off their bus and begun to explore Essex Street and all the shops there. By the time I was done assisting them in locating the various tinctures and elixirs they wanted, half an hour had passed, and Sage emerged from the break room to ask if I was ready to have my lunch.

Luckily, all the activity had gotten my appetite going again, and I was all too glad to relinquish the cash register to her and allow myself some quiet time. Once I was done with my sandwich and had finished my iced tea, my sunny outlook on life had returned.

Business was good, and I was going over to Noah's house tonight for an impromptu barbecue. I'd actually been doing a lot of that lately, since— even though I was a whiz at creating potions and elixirs, and spent a good deal of time in the kitchen working with my cauldrons—I'd never been much for cooking. The newly renovated backyard at Noah's rented house was the perfect venue for him to show off his skills with the barbecue...and also for us to enjoy the lovely summer weather, something we knew was all too short in our part of the world.

Derek Falco's unexpected request had been a blip on the radar, nothing more. I needed to push the incident out of my mind and concentrate on all the good times ahead with Noah.

As I often did, I brought Milo with me that night. Early on, Noah had let me know I was welcome to have my newly adopted dog join us whenever I went over to his house, and Milo, who adored Noah, was always happy to come along.

Right now, the cocker spaniel was sitting near the barbecue, tail wagging as he watched Noah transfer some marinated chicken skewers and separate skewers of veggies to the grill. No, Milo wasn't too interested in fire-roasted red peppers or zucchini, but he'd never met a piece of grilled chicken he didn't like.

"How was work?" Noah asked. He had on his usual black apron covering that day's chambray shirt and jeans, and, as usual, his thick, wavy brown hair looked a little mussed.

Which didn't matter one bit. Noah Jenkins was drop-dead gorgeous no matter what, with his bright blue eyes and friendly, even features. He looked good even with bedhead and two days' growth of beard.

Actually, to be honest, he looked even more spectacular when he was all rumpled.

"Fine," I said, and sipped some of the rosé he'd

poured for me a few minutes earlier. "Busier than I'd thought it would be for a Wednesday, because we got a couple of tour buses. It looks like this summer is shaping up to be a good one."

Especially now that things seemed to have gone quiet again, thank God. After dealing with two murders practically back to back, I was ready for my world to resume its usual uneventful rhythm. That might have sounded strange for someone who was a practicing witch, but really, except for having a few special talents, being a witch didn't make you all that much different from anyone else. You still had to get out of bed each morning and go to work, had to pay your taxes and schedule cleanings at the dentist and do all the hundred and one other things that composed most people's everyday lives.

And, while I loved working with other witches' familiars, I was also glad things had been quiet on that front as well. That was a sort of sideline for me —in addition to owning Full Moon Apothecary, I'd also been born with the peculiar talent of being able to talk to familiars. Because of that gift, sometimes witches came to me when they were having trouble with their animal companions and needed someone to act as an intermediary, so to speak. That was how Milo had entered my life, when his mistress, Darla Fitzgerald, was having problems because he wouldn't talk.

In the end, it had turned out Milo wasn't speaking because Darla herself had cast a spell on him to give her an excuse to bring him to me and keep him safely out of the way of the man she'd been seeing—a man who'd turned out to have witch blood, along with a terrible shape-shifting talent—but still, Milo was only one in a long line of familiars I'd worked with. He'd ended up staying permanently because of his mistress's untimely death, but in general, a familiar would be with me for a week, maybe a little more, until I could get their particular problems sorted out and send them back to their mistresses.

"Oh, and I got an update on Cinny," I added, naming the ginger cat who stayed with me only a few weeks earlier. She'd longed for a family, but couldn't have one because familiars by their very nature were sterile. "Her owner sent me a photo."

Noah turned away from the grill, expression alive with curiosity, and I picked up my phone from the spot where it had been resting on the tabletop and showed him the picture Doris had sent earlier that afternoon. True, Cinnamon couldn't have babies of her own, but she'd ended up fostering some kittens whose mother had been killed—and nursing them as well, thanks to a potion I'd whipped up for her. I'd explained the potion away by telling Noah it was something I'd originally made for a lactation coach over in

Marblehead, and luckily, he hadn't asked too many
questions.

Anyway, the photo showed an obviously happy
Cinny with two of the kittens nursing, while the
other two—a gray tabby and the little calico girl
who'd stolen my heart—wrestled with each other
in the foreground. Noah smiled at once, face bright
as the sun that had begun to slip toward the
horizon.

"She looks like she's doing great."

"She is," I assured him. "Her owner says the
kittens are getting bigger every day, but she's
decided to keep all of them. That way, Cinnamon
can have her family with her forever."

Well, nearly forever. Familiars lived as long as
their human companions and passed almost as
soon as their witches were gone. Milo was an excep-
tion to that rule, probably because his connection
to Darla had never been very strong. But even
though cats could live seventeen or eighteen years
or longer, those little kittens still probably
wouldn't outlast Cinnamon, whose mistress was a
vigorous witch in her early sixties.

However, Noah didn't know anything about
all that, so he simply appeared even more cheerful
at my report. "That's great news," he said. "The
world needs more of those kinds of happy
endings."

That was for sure. I couldn't help reflecting

that neither Darla Fitzgerald nor Trevor Miller had had their own happy endings, although, at least in those cases, their killers had met with some kind of justice. Thad Miller had taken his own life, and Brian Alatorre, the man who'd murdered Darla, had died of a stroke while in police custody.

Not of natural causes, though. No one in my coven had spoken of it openly, but I was pretty sure that Elise Figg, a witch about twenty years my senior, had cast some sort of spell to make sure Brian died quietly in his sleep. Elise was rumored to dabble in dark magic, something that was frowned upon if not outright forbidden, and definitely wouldn't have volunteered any information even if I'd asked her point-blank whether she'd done something to make sure he was safely out of the way.

Because Brian had been an abomination. Witches always had female children, never boys, because something about our magic became twisted when it encountered a Y-chromosome, making those children into terrible shapeshifters who couldn't be controlled. However, Brian's mother hadn't known she was carrying a boy along with his twin sister, and hadn't cast the proper spells to keep him from coming to term. When he was born, she'd sent him away to be raised by a regular couple—mundies, mundane folk—and he'd grown into his awful powers with no one to guide him. There were probably many in our community who would have said his death was a blessing, but still, it wasn't anything any of us wanted to talk about.

As best I could, I pushed those dark recollections aside, and made myself smile.

"Yes," I told Noah, "the world needs as many happy endings as it can get."

Chapter 2

Hedging Your Bets

I HADN'T PLANNED TO STAY LATE AT Noah's house, as it was a weeknight and we both had to be up early the next morning. Noah especially, since his clinic hours began at eight while Full Moon Apothecary didn't open until ten. Just as well, because I got a call the next morning at only a little before nine, something that made me frown in annoyance.

Even my mother knew not to call me before ten in the morning unless it was an utter emergency.

The number on my iPhone's screen wasn't familiar, and I was half-tempted to ignore the call and let it roll over to voicemail.

On the other hand, while I wasn't exactly on call the way a doctor—or a veterinarian—might be, I was also in the peculiar position of offering a very special service to the witch community, one that came with its own set of weird hours.

I released a sigh, told myself I should be glad that at least the call had come in after I'd showered and had breakfast and coffee, and picked up the phone.

"This is Charity Hughes."

"Oh, hi." A woman's voice, kind of breathless, definitely no one I knew. "I'm so sorry to bother you this early, but it's kind of an emergency."

"What kind of emergency?" I asked, although I thought I probably already knew the answer to that question. Whoever this woman was, she must be having trouble with her familiar.

"It's Lionel," she said, then added, "My hedgehog."

Hedgehog? That was a new one. Witches had familiars of all shapes and sizes—although they were always a breed that could easily be managed in someone's house—but I'd never heard of a hedgehog familiar before. "Are you having problems with him?"

"Oh, no," the woman replied at once. "He's a wonderful familiar. The problem is, I'm about to get married."

Why should that be a problem? I managed to respond, "Um...congratulations."

"Thank you," the woman said. "Oh, I'm Sela, by the way. Sela Warren. No, the problem is that

Colin and I were just about to leave for Cancun—we're getting married there—and the airline told me I couldn't bring Lionel. Something about him not being a domesticated animal, or whatever."

I made a sympathetic sound. Yes, this was the sort of problem witches encountered whose familiars weren't more common animals like cats and dogs. However, one would think Sela might have tried to make accommodations for her companion sometime during the planning stages of her destination wedding.

"Anyway," she went on in that same breathless voice, not giving me time to say anything in reply, "I was really hoping you could watch Lionel while Colin and I are out of the country. I know it's not exactly the kind of thing you usually do, but since you're used to working with familiars...."

The words trailed off, their implication clear enough. Maybe this wasn't the same thing as working out any issues a familiar and their mistress might have, but Sela seemed to think that didn't matter, that I could offer some kind of glorified pet-sitting.

I might have been annoyed...except I'd discussed doing almost that same exact thing just a few weeks ago with Milo and Cinnamon, who'd suggested I might offer the service as a way for witches and familiars to take a vacation from each other, so to speak. The bond between a witch and her animal companion was generally very strong, but that didn't mean it might not help for them to take a break now and then.

That was probably why I didn't hesitate as I said, "I can do that for you, Sela. When would you need to drop Lionel off?"

"Later this morning," she said immediately. "Our flight leaves at two."

Nothing like cutting it close. But I didn't know the woman and didn't want to waste time on nitpicking her apparent lack of advance planning, so I only replied, "How about ten?"

"We'll be there," she promised.

After that, I gave her my address, said I was looking forward to meeting her and Lionel, and ended the call. I didn't put down the phone, though. No, instead I started composing a text to Sage.

It looks like I'm going to be a little late this morning....

Sela Warren appeared to be around my own age of twenty-nine, although definitely more glamorous than I could ever hope to be. Her sleek dark hair contrasted with my wild mane of long red waves, and she was wearing a knee-length sheath dress in a shade of cobalt blue that I knew I'd never be brave enough to wear.

"Thank you so much," she said as she handed —more like thrust—a pretty brass cage over to me, along with a bag of kibble.

Inside the cage was Lionel, a tiny ball of spines almost small enough to fit in the palm of my hand, and who looked out at me with bright black eyes but didn't seem inclined to speak. Maybe he was shy around strangers.

"Oh, it's nothing," I replied, even as I hoped those words weren't anything more than the truth. After all, how hard could it be to look after a hedgehog? "You said you'd be gone for ten days?"

"Yes," she said. Her gaze appeared to scan the room, although there wasn't much to see except the shabby jumble of furniture I'd put together over the years. Maybe she was just trying to assess whether there was anything in the space that might pose a hazard for her diminutive familiar. "We'll be back the evening of the twenty-fifth, so I can pick up Lionel the next morning."

Technically making her familiar's stay eleven days long, but I didn't bother to point that out.

Milo was standing nearby, looking on with interest, although he knew better than to say anything. Not that Sela would have been able to understand him, since witches could only communicate with their own familiars and not anyone else's animal companions.

"Just call me when you're ready to come get him, and I'll have him ready," I promised.

"Perfect," she said, with another one of those almost nervous glances around the room. "But now I really need to get going. Colin's waiting for me."

She waved at her familiar, then practically ran for the door, far more steady on her high-heeled sandals than I ever would have been.

It seemed like an awfully unceremonious leave-taking when she wouldn't be seeing her familiar again for almost two weeks, but maybe she still had a lot of packing to do. I couldn't say I knew Sela Warren at all well, and yet she already struck me as the type of person who liked to do everything at the last minute.

I looked down at the cage I held, then set it on the floor before opening the tiny door that led inside. "Well, Lionel," I said, "I guess it's time we got acquainted."

The hedgehog seemed so disinclined to speak that at first I was worried he'd been hexed the way Milo had been, and I'd have to figure out a way to break the spell. But after he'd wandered around the kitchen, sniffed at Milo's bowl, and investigated the wood floor beneath the table off to one side, he paused and gave a satisfied nod.

"I like this place," he announced. He had a squeaky little voice, higher than I'd expected it to be. Then again, this was my first experience with a hedgehog familiar, so it wasn't as though I had much previous data to go on.

I tried not to look too amused. "I'm glad," I said. "Since this is going to be your home for the next little bit."

Lionel looked over at Milo, who'd been waiting off to one side, clearly wanting to give this latest— if temporary—addition to our household plenty of personal space. "Are you Charity's familiar?"

Because, while I'd introduced myself and Milo right off the bat after Sela had left, I hadn't gone into a lot of explanations, figuring discussing the dynamics of our home would give the two creatures a nice, neutral topic for their first conversation.

"No," Milo replied. Unlike Lionel, he had a deep voice, almost gravelly in its timbre, like most of the dog familiars I'd met. "My mistress passed away, and Charity took me in."

Lionel's tiny, pointed nose wrinkled. "But I thought we familiars go when our witches do."

"Mostly, that's true," I cut in, but gently. I could tell from the way Milo's golden-brown forehead had wrinkled that he wasn't quite sure of the best way to respond to our guest's comment. "But there were extenuating circumstances in Milo's case."

To my relief, Lionel didn't seem too interested in pursuing the matter further. Instead, he started sniffing around the kitchen again, surprising me by pausing so he could roll around on the spot where I'd spilled some carnation oil earlier that morning, even though I'd done my best to wipe it up.

Clearly, though, the little hedgehog could still smell traces of the oil, and was fascinated by it. He wriggled in the spot, eyes closed in apparent bliss, as he tried his best to get as much of the scent as possible all over him. Then he stood up and brushed at his quills, and sent me a lopsided little smile.

"Sorry," he said. "I just love smells. But I won't do that if it bothers you. Sela's used to it."

"You do whatever makes you feel comfortable," I assured him. After getting the call from his mistress, I'd hopped onto Google to acquaint myself with at least the rudiments of having a hedgehog as a pet, so I knew that "anointing" themselves was a big deal for the tiny creatures. At least Lionel had only rolled around in some leftover carnation oil, which was relatively harmless.

However, I could tell Lionel differed from his hedgehog brethren in that he seemed fully awake and active at ten-something in the morning, even though hedgehogs were nocturnal creatures who spent their daylight hours fast asleep. Just another quirk of being a familiar, I supposed; while some witches I knew were definitely night owls, most of them shared the same basic schedule as anyone who had a regular nine-to-five job.

"Would you like to go outside?" I suggested. "Milo can show you around the yard."

This idea obviously appealed to both creatures, because Milo's tail started wagging and Lionel's adorable little ears perked right up. Even though I had a doggy door installed right next to the kitchen's back entrance, I went ahead and opened the "people" door, as the dog called it, and let the two of them outside. Lionel scampered along behind Milo as he tried to keep up with the cocker spaniel's much longer strides.

While I knew my backyard was perfectly safe— well, now that Brian Alatorre was no longer a threat—I stood on the stoop, figuring it was probably better to keep an eye on the two critters, if only to see how they got along together. I didn't get as much of a feeling of instant rapport as I had when Cinnamon stayed with us, but I also hadn't noted any animosity between Milo and our latest familiar guest. Most likely, it was just that the two of them were so very different that it was going to take a little longer for them to become fast friends.

I could see immediately that Lionel wanted to stop and smell just about everything, pausing here and there to roll around in the grass whenever he encountered a scent that appeared particularly interesting.

Here's hoping that wasn't where Milo peed last, I thought, my mouth quirking despite itself.

Even if it was, cleaning up the hedgehog shouldn't be too much work. I'd heard that mild, soapy water and a soft toothbrush would work wonders on his quills.

I also reflected it was a good thing Sage and I had already agreed that I should stay home today. She'd told me I shouldn't leave Lionel alone on his first day here, and since it was a Thursday, she doubted the store would be so busy that she wouldn't be able to manage things by herself.

Of course, I'd thanked her, and told her I'd be in for sure the next day. Maybe she was feeling better than usual about the situation because I'd given her a hefty raise just the week before, but at the same time, I didn't want her to think that I considered the raise *carte blanche* to come in whenever I felt like it. The store was mine, not hers, and even though having to babysit a familiar threw a monkey wrench into things from time to time, it still shouldn't prevent me from being there as much as I possibly could.

After about fifteen minutes or so, Milo and

Lionel came back up the steps and into the kitchen, with Lionel announcing he was hungry.

"Right on it," I told him, and went to get the bag of cat food Sela had brought for him. My research had told me that hedgehogs liked bugs—caterpillars and mealworms and such—but she hadn't mentioned anything about that.

Maybe the little guy had grabbed a quick snack in the backyard when I wasn't looking.

For now, though, he seemed content with the small bit of cat food I poured into a bowl for him. Unlike Doris Dalrymple, Cinnamon's mistress, Sela hadn't seemed very prepared when she brought Lionel to the house, and had only handed over the bag of cat food and his cage. I supposed she must have been distracted by all the hubbub surrounding her destination wedding, although, since she'd dropped her familiar off on a Thursday, it seemed to me she was cutting it close if she was going to get married this coming weekend. Wouldn't she still have a lot of things to handle once she got to Cancun?

Who knows. It was entirely possible that she'd gotten a better deal on her tickets and accommodations by starting her wedding trip on a Thursday, rather than arriving the weekend before.

Because yes, most witches used regular means to get around—planes, trains, and automobiles. We all rode broomsticks, but some of us were better at it than others. However, even the best broomstick rider in the world...like my friend Stella Monroe, who'd won the gold medal in broomstick riding at the Witch Olympics multiple years in a row before she hung up her broom once she got pregnant... couldn't lug along a fiancé and all the luggage necessary to accommodate a ten-day trip to Cancun.

Anyway, it was a little bit of a mystery, but not that big a one.

Since Lionel seemed occupied with his early lunch—or maybe it was a late breakfast, considering how scattered Sela had seemed when she dropped him off—and Milo appeared content to hunker down a few feet away from our houseguest, I decided I might as well whip up a batch of my insomnia elixir, which was one of my shop's most popular items and almost always needed replenishing.

I stepped around the hedgehog, got out my cauldron and filled it with water before setting it on the stove, and then began gathering the necessary ingredients—chamomile, valerian, cherry juice. After I set them on the counter, I reached over and turned the dial to switch on the gas.

Only to have a blue flame shoot out from under the cauldron, reaching at least a foot in every direction. Luckily, I had good reflexes, so I was able to jump out of the way and only singed a couple of arm hairs.

Unfortunately, my bundles of dried valerian and chamomile didn't fare so well, and instantly burst into flame. I retained just enough presence of mind to cry out a quick fire-suppression spell.

Begone, fire
Don't raise my ire!

At once, the flames subsided, and I gave a relieved blink.

"Is everything okay?" Lionel asked, and I turned to see him standing next to his now-empty bowl, pointy little face the picture of concern. Next to him, Milo stared at me in worry, although he seemed to relax slightly when he realized I hadn't suffered any serious damage.

"It's fine," I said. "Just a minor hiccup with the stove."

Even as the words left my mouth, though, I wondered how such a thing could have happened. Most of my house was decorated in a generally charming mishmash of antiques and hand-me-downs, furniture I knew wouldn't get ruined by the parade of familiars that came through my home, but the stove was a top-of-the-line Wolf I'd had installed a few years earlier when I redid the kitchen. I'd justified the splurge by telling myself I needed something that fancy to make sure all my potions and elixirs came out the way I intended them to, although the purchase had put a pretty decent dent in my remodeling budget.

At any rate, the chances of my 2012 Land Rover Discovery exploding were much higher than the odds of my high-end oven doing the same thing, which made me wonder just what the hell was going on. Had I accidentally left the gas on the last time I'd used the stovetop?

That didn't make much sense. I was always really careful about that sort of thing, mostly because I worked with a lot of herbs, and the last thing I needed was the items I'd carefully gathered in my garden going up in flames, just like the valerian and the chamomile had a few minutes earlier.

However, since I couldn't come up with a reasonable explanation for what else might have happened, I had to chalk this one up to user error… even though I hadn't smelled gas before my stove decided to perform a reenactment of the *Hindenburg* explosion.

And to prove to the two familiars that I wasn't rattled, I calmly knocked the scorched herbs into the trash, wiped down the countertop, and went to my pantry to get more chamomile and valerian. Luckily, the cherry juice was kept in a glass bottle, and it had survived the explosion just fine.

The second batch of the elixir went together

without incident, so I told myself it was just one of those things.

Even so, I couldn't quite shake the feeling that something was very wrong here.

That night I knew I was going to have a quiet night at home, since Noah had already told me he planned to drive down to Boston to have dinner with his family. A part of me had wanted to ask why he hadn't invited me along, although I knew it was way too early in our relationship for the whole "meet the parents" thing. Our connection felt very strong, but it had still been less than a month since we started seeing each other seriously, and I knew I needed to wait.

After all, he hadn't met my mother, either, and she lived right here in Salem.

I supposed I should be grateful for small favors.

Oh, I loved my mother. She was an amazing woman...and a powerful witch. Obviously, she knew I was dating Noah and was thrilled about it, but she hadn't pushed for a family dinner yet, probably because this relationship had come about after a long dry spell in my personal life and she didn't want to do anything that might jeopardize it.

I supposed I should give her credit for that

much; even Amelia Hughes knew that sometimes she could come on just a little too strong.

Anyway, it was probably a good thing I was home, since that meant Lionel wouldn't be left alone on his first evening here. Milo would have kept him company, of course, but it still seemed better for me to be around, even if I couldn't guarantee that I'd stay in every night during the rest of his tenure at my house.

I heated some leftover chili and ate it at the kitchen table, with Miles and Lionel having their own dinners from their bowls only a few feet away. That part of the evening was completely uneventful—the microwave didn't explode, and I didn't choke on a piece of ground beef or anything close to it. No, I ate my leftovers, and did my best to collect some information from Lionel regarding his mistress.

"Has she been engaged for very long?" I asked, which seemed like an innocent enough question.

"No," the hedgehog replied in his squeaky little voice. "She only met Colin a month ago."

I couldn't quite prevent my eyes from widening. "A month?"

He nodded, and ate a piece of the small chunk of apple I'd put in his bowl, after he'd confided in me that he actually did like fruit quite a bit. "Yes. I told her I thought that was awfully fast, especially with how witches are."

There was an understatement. Everyone in the witch world knew you had to be absolutely, positively sure that anyone we invited into our lives was the person we planned to spend the rest of our lives with. Otherwise, we were taking way too big a risk of letting the wrong man—or woman—be privy to secrets that could spell disaster for the entire community if they were ever revealed.

"What did she say to that?" Milo inquired then, obviously intrigued by the conversation as well. Maybe he was contrasting Sela's behavior with mine; I'd known Noah for around a year and had been intimate with him for several weeks, but there was no way in the world I would ever have let slip the tiniest hint that there was more to me—or my mother, or Sage, or Stella, or anyone else in my circle—than met the eye.

Lionel let out the tiniest little sigh. "She said it was none of my business. I told her of course it was, since I was her familiar, but she just shook her head and said I didn't understand."

In a way, Sela had a point there. Because familiars were meant to be with their mistresses for their entire lives, and having families of their own would have only been a distraction, they were always sterile, and never seemed to have any inclination to develop romantic relationships with other members of their species. Because of that, it seemed plausible enough that Lionel would have a very hard time understanding the passion that had apparently flamed between his mistress and her new husband.

However, pointing out any of that didn't seem very diplomatic to me, so I only shrugged and said, "Well, the heart wants what it wants, I suppose."

The hedgehog gave what looked like an echoing lift of his tiny shoulders, but he didn't contradict me. No, he only returned to the piece of apple I'd given him while I went ahead and finished my chili.

Afterward, we all headed into the living room, where I picked up the remote for the television. Milo and Cinny had enjoyed watching *Animal Planet* together, so I thought that would be a good way to spend the rest of the evening. Just a quiet night in and an early bedtime. Tomorrow was Friday, and although Noah and I didn't have any concrete plans yet, I wanted to make sure I was rested for whatever we ended up doing for the weekend.

As soon as I pressed the button to turn on the TV, however, the screen exploded in a shower of sparks. Shocked, I dropped the remote, even as the two familiars scrambled to the relative safety of the rear of the couch, obviously hoping its bulk would protect them.

However, after that first explosion, the screen only went dark, and didn't seem inclined to indulge in any further pyrotechnics. Knees wobbly, I got up from the couch and went over to the TV.

"Are you sure you should do that?" Milo asked, sticking his head out from behind the sofa. "What if it explodes again?"

"I think it's done doing whatever it was going to do," I replied, glad I sounded a lot steadier than I felt...although that didn't stop me from unplugging the television just to be safe.

A brief inspection didn't show any obvious reason for my almost-new Samsung to have self-immolated. Then again, I was a witch, not a TV technician, so I had no idea exactly what I was supposed to be looking for.

"It's okay," I announced. "I mean, the TV's a goner, but it doesn't look like it's going to catch fire or anything. And it's still under warranty, so I should be able to get it replaced without too much trouble."

"What's a warranty?" Lionel asked, sharp little nose poking out next to Milo's golden-brown snout.

I did my best not to smile. "It's like an insurance policy. Do you know what that is?"

He gave a solemn nod.

"Well, it's like that, but for electronics or appliances or whatever. The TV is really new, so the warranty still covers it, which means I won't have to pay for a new television."

"Oh, that's good," he replied, his expression obviously relieved.

"It might be a while until I can get a new one, though," I went on. "So, it looks like it's a quiet reading night for me. You two okay with that?"

This time, both familiars nodded, and then crept cautiously out from behind the couch.

It was a quiet evening—too quiet, even though I got out my phone and streamed some quiet jazz from Spotify through the bluetooth speaker that sat on one of the bookshelves that flanked the fireplace. The whole time, I couldn't keep my thoughts from racing, even as I pretended to work my way through a James Patterson mystery and Milo and Lionel slept curled up on the rug in front of the hearth.

Two accidents like this, right after Lionel got here?

Coincidence, I tried to tell myself.

Somehow, though, I knew it was much more than that.

Chapter 3

Hex Marks the Spot

Reluctantly, I left the two familiars at home and headed off to work the next morning. I supposed I could have brought them to the shop —Milo had already proved he could last an entire workday at the store, and Lionel was so small I doubted he'd be much of a problem—but I worried that the trail of mishaps which appeared to have accompanied the hedgehog might follow him to Full Moon Apothecary, and it just seemed safer to have him stay put. My homeowner's insurance should take care of any other issues that cropped up...I hoped...but I really didn't want to put Sage or any of my customers at risk.

Especially when, as I was coming down the stairs to put the kettle on that morning, I tripped on the third step from the bottom and went flying. Luckily, I landed on the rug in the entryway and only had some scraped elbows and banged-up knees to show for my trouble, but still, that additional incident seemed to provide further evidence that something very strange was going on.

"You think it's another hex?" Sage asked after I related my tale of woe to her that morning at work. She was about seven years younger than I, with silky light brown hair and clear hazel eyes that always reminded me of a forest pool. "Like Darla Fitzgerald put on Milo to keep him from talking?"

The thought had already crossed my mind, so about all I could do was say, "Maybe. I don't know. I didn't have time to try casting some spells to see."

Which was only the truth. I'd overslept and had rushed this morning, so I supposed it was possible that my tumble down the stairs had everything to do with my own clumsiness and distraction, and nothing more.

Sage lifted an eyebrow, and I added, "On the surface, it doesn't make a lot of sense. I mean, Darla cast that silencing spell on Milo to give her an excuse to bring him to me but at the same time keep him from telling me anything incriminating. But why would Sela do that to Lionel? I'd already agreed to take him in during her trip. If anything, she'd want to cast a spell to make him the luckiest hedgehog in the world so I'd be more inclined to keep him longer if necessary."

This argument seemed to hit home, because

my assistant nodded. "That's true. So...maybe Sela has enemies we don't know about."

Which was entirely possible. After all, I didn't know much about the woman, except she lived in Marblehead—the neighboring town—was around thirty, and apparently impetuous enough to marry someone she'd only known for a month. Although Salem and Marblehead were located right next to each other, allowing witches from both communities to go back and forth all the time...Noah and I ended up there at least a couple of times a month, since one of his favorite breweries was located there...they had their own covens, their own witch community. We really weren't involved in each other's business very much.

"Well, that would explain why she'd been in such a hurry to get to Cancun," I said.

Sage's mouth curled in an ironic smile. "Yeah, maybe she stole someone's boyfriend, and that was why she was in so much of a rush to get out of the country."

The thought hadn't even crossed my mind, but the theory made some sense. If Sela really had poached another witch's significant other, then I could see why the hexes had started flying. In general, witches tried to avoid using magic that was too showy, lest we attracted the wrong kind of attention, but in matters of the heart, common sense often went right out the window.

"You'd think they'd hex Sela herself instead of her poor hedgehog," I said slowly, and Sage just shrugged.

"I don't know how it all works, because I don't have a familiar," she replied. "But maybe putting a hex on a witch's familiar hurts her even more than if the curse was directed right at her."

Although I worked with a lot of familiars, I had to admit I still wasn't entirely knowledgeable about all the dynamics involved. Complicating things further was the simple fact that every witch had a slightly different relationship with her animal companion, so it was even more difficult to quantify all their interactions. If Sela was the kind of witch who leaned heavily on her familiar to assist her with spellwork, then I could see why going after Lionel might have caused even more disruption than usual.

"Well," I said, "I guess the first thing I need to do is find out if I'm really dealing with a hex at all."

Sage's mouth quirked again. "Need me to cover the store?"

Her expression was too amused for the words to come across as resigned, but I'd already told myself that I was going to do my damnedest to make sure I didn't keep abandoning her every time there was a crisis. Noah had texted me on my way to work, asking if I wanted to go out to Mercy Tavern tonight, and I let him know it might be better if we just had takeout at my place, since someone had dropped off a new animal foster for me the day before. We'd agreed on pizza, and for him to come over around seven, which gave me plenty of time to get to the bottom of this hex problem before he even showed up.

"No, that's okay," I said firmly. "I'll look into it after work."

Lately, I'd been expanding my magical repertoire slightly by working on scrying and getting better at Tarot, but this was still something that seemed pretty far outside my wheelhouse. Although my mother was a powerful witch, I didn't want her over at the house when there was a chance Noah might show up early, and that was why I called Grace Bowersby and asked her if she could meet me at my place at five-thirty.

Grace was seven or eight years older than my mother, putting her in her late sixties. Her two daughters were both grown and had moved to Boston and joined covens there, which was why she had plenty of time to spend offering advice and insight to anyone who might ask. Before I was even born, she'd taken on the unofficial role of historian and accumulator of witchy knowledge here in

Salem, making her the perfect person to come over and offer her own insight into my current problem.

Now she stared down at Lionel, who sat on the hearthrug, looking blissfully unaware that he was the center of so much concern.

"He's adorable," Grace said. She was a plump woman with gray hair she often wore in a bun or pulled back in a ponytail, and today she had on one of her signature neon-bright outfits—hot pink capri pants, a pink and lime green sleeveless top, and green sandals adorned with pink and green rhinestones—making her once again look like one of the least witchy women in the world.

"He is," I replied, as the hedgehog rolled over onto his back, feet tucked against his little white tummy. "His cuteness isn't the problem, though. It's whether or not someone was mean enough to hex him."

Her eyes narrowed. They were bright blue, slightly obscured by oval pink-framed glasses. "Well, that's easy enough to find out."

She squatted down with surprising ease, considering her age and weight, and put a hand over the tiny animal, although she didn't try to touch him. His round black eyes blinked up at her in surprise, but because he was a familiar and used to working with witches, he didn't try to get away, only remained lying there on the rug.

. . .

Hedgehog small, so sweet and kind,
    In lamplight's glow, your fate I bind.
    If hexed you be, reveal the sign,
    Of wicked spell so unkind.

After Grace was done with the incantation, a strange reddish glow surrounded the hedgehog for a second or two before dissipating into pale pink twinkles. She shook her head, then straightened into a standing position with a little less dexterity than she'd shown when kneeling down a minute earlier.

"Someone's definitely placed a hex on him," Grace said. "As far as I can tell, it was designed to attract general misfortune, which explains the gas explosion in your kitchen and the TV blowing up —and your fall down the stairs."

I glanced down at one of my elbows, exposed by my sleeveless black summer dress. It was definitely red and had a few obvious scrapes, but it could have been worse.

Much worse.

"So...not to kill," I said. To some people, that might have seemed like a big leap, but considering I'd dealt with two different murder cases in just the last month, I didn't think it too strange that my brain had immediately gone to that particular scenario.

"Not as far as I can tell," Grace replied. She shook her head, expression troubled. "Even so, it's a terrible thing to place a spell on a witch's familiar, since the little creatures are innocents. It's not as if the familiar himself would have done something to invite such cruelty."

While I agreed with that sentiment, I couldn't help responding, "Well, as far as I can tell, nothing bad has happened to Lionel so far. Everything seemed to happen to the closest witch in the vicinity, namely me."

"True," Grace allowed, although she still looked worried. "But familiars are intimately connected to their witches. Any pain they suffer, the familiar experiences as well, if to a lesser degree. The only reason none of these mishaps affected Lionel is that you're not his witch."

No, I wasn't. I was only a woman trying to understand why someone would do something so awful to him...and, by extension, to Sela Warren.

"Do you know who did this?" I asked next. It was kind of a long shot, but sometimes an especially talented witch could tell who had cast a particular spell, and Grace was nothing if not talented.

But she only shook her head. "No," she said. "The witch who created this hex was very good at covering her tracks. Sometimes, I can recognize magic cast by the others in our coven—your mother, Valerie, Tonya, Elise—but this doesn't feel like any of them."

And there wasn't any reason why it should. None of them knew Sela, or had any reason to hurt her or her familiar. Not even Elise Figg, who was the only one of us to ever dabble in the darker borders of the magic we all used.

It had been a long shot even to ask, but I couldn't help feeling discouraged. If a witch was capable of casting a spell like this, what else might she be capable of?

I had one more request to make, though.

"Can you remove the hex?"

For a long moment, Grace was silent. Then she shook her head. "By myself, no. It's possible the coven working together could do something to lift it. Should I call a meeting?"

I hesitated. By that point, it was almost six-thirty, and I knew Noah would be over in a half an hour, maybe a little more. There really wasn't time to have the coven gather, not at this short notice. And although we'd kept our plans hazy beyond having him come over for pizza, I knew both of us were imagining the evening ending in my bedroom.

Well, that wasn't going to happen. I wouldn't cancel, not at this late date, but at the same time, I'd just have to maneuver things so he'd go home fairly soon after we ate—a manufactured story about having to go in to the shop early the next morning to do inventory, something plausible that wouldn't have him question me too closely.

Because the last thing I wanted was to have Noah start investigating exactly what I was really up to.

To my infinite relief, when I told him I had to be at the store at seven the next day, Noah looked disappointed but understanding.

"I get it," he said as he pulled a small piece of pepperoni off his pizza and handed it to a waiting Milo, whose tail wagged with ferocious glee. "I've got a surgery scheduled at eight, so we can both plan to be good little children tonight."

"Thanks," I said, hoping the relief in my voice wasn't too obvious. "I can stay up as late as I want tomorrow night."

His bright blue eyes took on a familiar glint. "I'm going to hold you to that."

"I hope you're going to hold me to a whole lot of things."

That comment made him grin, as I'd hoped it would, and the rest of our dinner continued without incident. Afterward, he kissed me goodbye, asked if I wanted to barbecue at his house the following night, and then headed to the driveway, where his Toyota Tundra was parked. I smiled and waved goodbye as he backed out onto the street... and then closed the door as soon as he'd gone around the corner.

Time to get to work.

Grace had already gotten out the word that there would be a coven meeting at her house that night, so all I had to do was send her a quick text to let her know I was on my way over, knowing she'd do the rest of the work to summon the troops.

Not that there were all that many of us. My mother, Grace Bowersby, Elise Figg, Izzy Halloran...Sage's mom...Tonya Willis, and Valerie Monroe, Stella's grandmother. It wasn't a huge coven, but all of us were good at what we did, so we didn't need the ritual twelve. In the past, Stella would sometimes join us, but with a newborn at home, she probably wouldn't be attending any more of these ceremonies for at least a year, if not more. And Sage was also part of our coven, although she also wasn't a regular participant.

Luckily, we didn't need to have Lionel there for us to remove the curse. The poor little guy was beginning to pick up that something bad had been done to him, but I assured him that everything was going to be taken care of and all he had to do was hang tight with Milo, who would keep an eye on things. The dog, who was naturally protective, told me he'd make sure both Lionel and the house would be fine, and I'd sent him a grateful smile, glad that he knew exactly what he needed to do.

No, since Grace had seen the hex for herself and knew how it was constructed, it was enough to have her lead the ceremony and direct the spell required to break the curse, and for the rest of us to lend her our strength. It was possible that the witch who'd created the enchantment in the first place was stronger than any of us individually, but I knew there was no way her spell could possibly stand up to the combined might of seven very determined coven members.

We stood in Grace's basement with its forest green walls and old oak floor underneath our feet, battery-powered candles flickering from the walls. Some of us still used the real thing, but she was fussy about her house and much preferred not to have to worry about wax dripping everywhere.

"Thank you for coming," I told everyone as we gathered in our circle. "I know this is kind of short notice."

"It's fine," Elise said. She had long dark hair— now streaked with gray—that she often wore in a French braid, and clear gray eyes that looked like ocean waters with a storm coming. "The important thing to do is get this hex lifted."

Tonya nodded. Like Elise, she was in her early fifties, but her brown hair didn't show a single silver strand. Maybe she used magic to keep the gray at bay, or maybe her hairstylist made sure her age didn't show in her shoulder-length bob. "Did you let Sela Warren know what was going on?"

"No," I said frankly. "I mean, I suppose at some point I'll text her or something to let her know we got rid of the hex, but since she didn't seem too worried about telling me that someone had cursed her familiar, I don't feel too obligated to be quick about it."

Across the circle from me, my mother frowned slightly. "Charity, that's not a very mature attitude to have."

"Maybe not," I replied. "But I'm not going to drop everything now to try calling Sela, so we might as well get on with this."

For just a moment, my mother looked as though she wanted to argue the point with me further. However, she seemed to realize we were all here to help Lionel, not discuss my personal feelings about Sela Warren, so she instead pulled in a breath and said, "All right."

An uncomfortable pause followed her response, as if everyone was waiting to make sure neither my mother nor I were going to exchange any more tart words on the subject. However, since it must have become clear to everyone there that we didn't have anything else to say, Grace spoke next.

"Join hands, please."

Her tone was almost too neutral, and I took

that as a sign that she wasn't too pleased with either my mother or me at the moment. I wouldn't let myself worry about it, though. This wasn't the first time the two of us had butted heads, and I doubted it would be the last.

Hex upon this hedgehog, now take flight,
    In the name of magic, with all our might.
    With whispered words and moonbeam's grace,
    We lift the curse from his tiny face.
    By herbs and charms, we break your spell,
    Hedgehog freed, and all is well.

White light flared in the room, garish against the green-painted walls, signaling that our powers had joined to banish the hex, and I allowed myself a single relieved breath. That seemed to be that.

In the next moment, though, the white light turned into jagged lines like miniature lightning bolts, ricocheting off the ceiling and walls. I don't know who let go first, but within a second or two, we'd all released one another's' hands and had dropped to the floor, each of us by instinct casting a little bubble of glowing protection around ourselves.

The rogue magic skated around the room several more times before dissipating. A long, heavy silence fell, and then I demanded,

"What the hell was that?"

Chapter 4

Home Protection

Slowly, Valerie Monroe and Tonya Willis pushed themselves off the floor, and the rest of us followed suit. Although those raging bolts of lightning didn't seem to have hurt any of us, I could tell we were all stunned and shaken.

The spell should have worked. One witch's enchantment shouldn't have been strong enough to withstand the combined strength of seven magical practitioners. And yet...it had been.

"So...Lionel is still hexed?" I asked.

Grace Bowersby and Valerie Monroe—the two oldest, most experienced witches present—exchanged a weighted glance.

"It would seem that way," Grace said. "I've never felt blowback like that before. This is...very strange."

There was an understatement.

"What could make something like that happen?" Tonya Willis put in. She reached up to touch her hair, as if to make sure her immaculate bob hadn't been singed during that awful little episode. Since she was one of those women who always looked perfectly put together, from her sleek gray hair to the tips of the high heels she wore day in and day out, getting knocked to the floor like that must have been particularly annoying for her.

"I have no idea," Valerie replied. "This is a new one for me, too. But because Grace is fairly certain our spell failed, I think you have to assume the hex is still in place."

Wonderful. What did it have in store for me next? A shattered mirror? A broken phone? How about a trip and fall down my cellar stairs, this time all the way to the bottom instead of just a few steps?

"But that doesn't mean you need to worry," my mother said hastily, and I shot her an incredulous look.

"If you'd seen my exploded TV, you might not be so quick to say something like that."

Valerie sent me a glance that wasn't quite quelling, but somewhere on the outskirts of the expression. "We know this has been difficult for you, Charity," she said. "But just because we can't lift the hex, it doesn't mean we won't be able to provide you with some protection. Right?"

And she fixed her gaze on the other members of the coven, all of whom made various sounds of agreement.

"Exactly," Grace chimed in. "A simple protection spell should do the trick."

On the surface, that sounded like a good idea. But....

"Maybe you can protect me," I said slowly. "What about Milo, though? Or anyone who comes over to my house?"

Because the absolute last thing I needed was for Noah to suffer any kind of mishap simply because he'd stopped by with a bag of takeout or something. True, he seemed to have survived tonight's pizza dinner just fine, but he hadn't been at the house for very long. What might have happened if he actually had stayed the night?

"Simple enough," my mother said briskly. "The spell will include you, your house, and anyone who visits there. But it's probably a good idea to make sure Lionel stays on your property, and that you don't bring him to work. There are too many people coming and going from the shop, and it could strain the spell."

Since I'd already decided it was better to keep Lionel at home, I didn't think that sort of restriction would be too much of a problem. "I can do that," I told her.

Which is why I ended up having the rest of the

coven weave a spell of protection for me and my home and garden, and everything in it. As they worked, a soft golden glow formed around my body, letting me know the magic was working and that this time, I wouldn't have to worry about it splintering into a bunch of laser-focused lightning bolts intent on doing the exact opposite of what the spell had intended.

Afterward, as we were all getting ready to go our separate ways, my mother drew me aside.

"I'm sorry if I was short with you," she said, her voice pitched low enough that it would be difficult for the others to overhear.

"That's okay," I replied. We'd had enough little tiffs over the years that I wasn't going to brood on this one. It had been a difference of opinion, nothing more. "I probably should have reached out to Sela. It's just that I have a feeling she already knew what was going on, and that's why she fobbed Lionel off on me. She didn't want anything to interfere with her wedding trip."

My mother's mouth compressed, but it was clear enough to me that she'd done the mental math on her own and had come to much the same conclusion. "Well," she said, her tone now brisk, very different from the undertone of a moment before, "I suppose that's neither here nor there, considering she's thousands of miles away and none of us can do very much about it."

No, we couldn't. There was only an hour's time difference between Salem and Cancun, and yet I got the feeling Sela would do her very best to make sure she wasn't available, even if I tried to call her.

"I'll just have to tough it out," I said, and summoned a smile. "Luckily, Lionel is an adorable little thing. None of this is his fault."

"No, it isn't," my mother replied. "And I know you'll take good care of him."

For as long as I'm able, I thought, although I knew better than to say anything like that out loud to the woman who'd raised me. She'd tell me to stop borrowing trouble, and that nothing bad was going to happen.

Scratch that.

Nothing *worse* was going to happen.

But my drive home was completely uneventful, and when I got up the next morning, I managed to make it down the stairs without tripping, and I turned on the stove without suffering another gas explosion.

That had to be a good sign, right?

Both the familiars could tell something was up, so I fortified myself with some coffee, then did my best to explain the situation. The further I got into my story, the more Lionel's furry little face drooped, until his whiskers were practically perpendicular to the floor.

"Sela would do that to you?" he said, his voice only a bit above a whisper.

"Well, I don't think it was intentional," I said hastily, even though deep down that was pretty much exactly what I thought. "I think she believed the hex was directed at her, so if she was out of the way, then anyone who was watching you would be safe."

A few feet away, Milo cocked his head to one side and sent me a very penetrating look. It seemed pretty clear to me that, even if the hedgehog was buying it, my adopted dog didn't believe a single thing I was saying.

However, since it was Milo, I also knew he'd keep his opinions to himself. After I'd given him a home—one that was much more fun and interesting than the one he'd come from—he seemed to think I walked on water. If I wanted to tell Lionel a few little white lies, then my cocker spaniel wouldn't interfere.

"Oh," the hedgehog said, and appeared to contemplate my words for a moment. "I suppose I can see that. Sela is so caring and giving about everyone."

Yes, especially men who propose to her after a month of dating, I thought dryly.

But since Lionel obviously worshipped his mistress, I wasn't about to say anything that might change his opinion. No, I only reiterated that Lionel would need to stay at home while I was at work, and that the two familiars would have to find their own ways to amuse themselves.

"Staying here isn't a problem," Milo put in. "The backyard is big enough to keep us busy all day."

That it was. My property encompassed a little more than an acre, with an extensive herb garden and a nice expanse of grass and some trees, just perfect for wandering or napping or anything in between. And Milo had lived with me long enough that he knew it very well, and could keep an eye on Lionel to make sure he didn't get into any trouble while roaming around the property.

"It's very nice," the hedgehog said in his piping little voice, and I supposed that was the end of that.

All the same, I couldn't quite ignore the unease that tightened my shoulders as I drove in to work that Saturday morning. Yes, the day so far had been blessedly uneventful, but could I really depend on it to stay that way?

I had to hope so. Saturdays were always my busiest days at the store, and if some calamity occurred, I'd have a hard time getting away. And that was only if I even learned something had gone wrong at the house. True, a week or so ago, I'd gotten a cheapie cell phone that I'd programmed to call my phone and my phone only, and showed Milo how to push the button to call me in case of emergency, but what would happen if the dog became incapacitated somehow?

That seemed like borrowing a whole lot of trouble, though. The spell the coven had cast the night before seemed to be holding just fine, and I knew Milo would be a great guardian for Lionel. And after I got through today, I had a day off before I had to come back to work, time I could use to investigate the hex further and see if there was any way I could trace it back to its source.

Namely, the hostile witch who must have cast it in the first place. I wasn't the confrontational type—the exact opposite, actually—but even a wimp like me had a few choice words for anyone who'd cast such a despicable spell on such a tiny, innocent creature.

As best I could, I pushed all that out of my head, telling Sage when I came in that everything was fine. She might have given me a very slight side-eye at my comment, as if she could detect something in my voice or expression that let her know things weren't quite as hunky-dory as I wanted her to believe, but at least she didn't ask any probing questions.

And, much to my relief, the day went smoothly and quickly enough. I did take a longer than usual lunch, just so I could go home and check on the two familiars, but when I got there, they were both napping under the shade of the big oak off to one side of the lawn, looking as though they didn't have a care in the world.

Maybe they didn't. Constant fretting and worrying was more us humans' speed.

I fed them both lunch, though, and headed back to the store feeling much lighter of heart than I'd started out that morning. It was so busy in the afternoon that I was very glad I'd mixed up some more insomnia elixir, because otherwise, I would have run out before Sage was able to close the shop doors at five after five.

"And here I thought we'd have a lull before we got to the Fourth of July," she remarked as she turned the key in the lock.

"Me, too," I replied. "But the weather's been gorgeous. I suppose that has a lot to do with it."

My comment wasn't even an exaggeration. The days had been sunny and warm but not hot, the breezes off the ocean delicious and just enough to make the air feel refreshing rather than brisk. No wonder so many people thought it was the perfect time to come and stroll Salem's historic streets, to shop and eat and visit the museums.

If only I could relax and enjoy the beautiful weather.

Despite my underlying unease, I hadn't

canceled my plans to go over to Noah's house and barbecue for dinner. I'd only be about ten minutes away from home, closer than I'd been at the store, and I told myself the entire day had been quiet and serene, not giving me any reason to think I needed to stay with the two familiars.

In fact, when I got back to the house around five-thirty, Milo said quietly to me, "Everything is fine. You don't need to worry about us."

"Was it that obvious?" I replied, knowing that I smiled a little as I asked the question.

"To me," he said. A pause as he looked over at Lionel, who was not much more than a tiny, spiky ball at the base of the oak tree, and then he added, "He's okay. I think he was a little upset earlier about what his mistress had done, but it looks like he's forgotten about it already. That doesn't surprise me too much—hedgehogs don't tend to hang on to things for very long."

Now my mouth quirked again. "I didn't know you were such an expert."

"Animals know things."

Milo's expression was so serious as he uttered those words that I knew I couldn't let my smile get any bigger. Besides, he was right. Animals did know things, sometimes long before we dense humans did.

I bent over to pat him on the head, and then

give him a good scratch behind his long, floppy ears. "You're a good dog, Milo."

"And you're a good mistress."

He didn't add, *Much better than Darla,* because that was something we both already knew. Then again, it was a pretty low bar.

But I had to admit I was feeling a little more relaxed as I drove over to Noah's house, and let even more of my tension go after a few sips of the merlot he handed me as we headed into the backyard.

"You looked like you could use it," he said.

"Busy day at the store," I replied, which was partly true. However, a lively day at work didn't tend to drain me, mostly because a lot of customers meant I had no reason to fret about my livelihood. It wasn't that I had to worry about Full Moon Apothecary going belly up anytime soon, but even so, I had my lean months here and there, mostly in the winter when the flow of tourists dropped drastically and I had to rely on my local customers to get me through until spring break.

"Well, you've got some time off now," Noah said. He was looking relaxed himself, in some cargo shorts and a Marblehead Brewery T-shirt, and he'd smelled amazing, all citrusy and fresh, when he kissed me as he let me into the house. Just gazing at him as I sipped merlot made me feel about a million times better.

I couldn't tell him that, while the shop wouldn't be open again until Monday morning, I still had plenty on my plate. Although I really didn't know how I was going to go about it, I knew I had to do something to track down the witch who'd put that hex on Lionel.

Would I ever feel comfortable enough with Noah to tell him the truth about me, about the world I lived in?

Maybe in a year, if things kept going the way they were now. I'd never had a relationship last that long, but then, I'd never been with anyone like Noah before.

And again I marveled at Sela Warren, committing herself to a man after only knowing him for a month. I could only hope it would all work out and she—and the rest of the witch community—wouldn't end up regretting her impetuosity.

"And thank God for that," I said in response to Noah's comment.

He grinned and then headed over to the barbecue, where a bunch of chicken breasts and legs, liberally coated in what he'd told me was his mother's secret sauce, were already sending off the most enticing scents. My stomach growled, but because a house finch had just started trilling boisterously in one of the trees off to one side, I doubted Noah heard it.

"How's your family?" I asked, hoping that

sounded like an innocuous enough topic of conversation...and not at all like I was just the teeniest, tiniest bit annoyed he hadn't invited me along to his family dinner.

"They're doing great," Noah said. If he'd noticed any edge to my tone, he didn't give any sign of it. "My dad just retired, so he's still kind of getting used to not working every day. But he's got lots of projects planned, and they're talking about maybe buying an RV and traveling during the winter, going out to Arizona or California or something."

That sounded like a lot of fun. Salem was absolutely beautiful at Christmas, but I had to admit that by the time the tail end of February rolled around, I was all too ready for green trees and blue skies. Unfortunately, we didn't get to enjoy spring until the end of April, so I just had to grit my teeth and get through it. I definitely didn't have the luxury of hopping into an RV and heading for warmer climes.

Before I could come up with a pleasantly neutral response to his comment, Noah went on, "My mom was kind of giving me grief about not bringing you to dinner."

"Oh?" I returned, hoping I sounded completely neutral and not at all invested in his mother's opinion of me.

He flipped a couple of chicken breasts, then

said, "Yes, she said you sounded like a very interesting person, and she could tell from the way I talked about you it was serious." From behind the open lid of the barbecue, his blue eyes caught mine, and held. "It is...isn't it?"

"I think so," I said, doing my best to sound level, calm, even though my heart had suddenly decided to speed up. "Well, you can take me next time."

His gaze didn't waver. "I will."

There it was, stated so simply. He wanted me to meet his parents, even though the two of us had only been seeing each other for a few weeks. I wondered then how much he'd told them about his ex-fiancée being arrested for Trevor Miller's murder, although the charges had been dropped early on, and she was completely exonerated after Trevor's father wrote a confession letter before taking his own life.

I had a feeling Noah had probably been pretty open about the whole mess, just because he was like that. When I'd first met Shelby, I was angry with him because I thought he'd been hiding things from me, but the real truth was that she'd been out of his life long enough that he hadn't really considered her a big deal.

Noah definitely wasn't the one in our relationship who was hiding a whole bunch of secrets.

But I smiled and said, "That sounds great," and

we went on to talk about other things, like possibly another trip on his friend Jared's boat the next weekend, and how Jared and Kathy were thinking about having a blowout Fourth of July barbecue at their house. Simple, ordinary topics...no hexes or familiars or witches who'd suddenly decided to elope to Cancun.

I liked it that way.

However, the witchy reality of my life intruded as soon as I got home. Milo met me at the door, looking worried.

"Lionel isn't feeling well," he told me.

At once, alarm flared. "What's wrong with him?"

"I don't know," Milo replied, leading me out of the entry and into the living room. "He seemed fine when we had our dinner around six, but then he started acting listless."

"Do you think it was something he ate?"

"It was just the same cat food he had before," Milo replied, his furry golden-brown forehead wrinkled with worry.

Lionel was curled up in a tiny ball on the hearthrug. I kneeled down next to him and reached out to gently stroke his spiny back.

"Hey, there," I said softly. "Milo says you're feeling a little off."

The hedgehog unrolled a little bit and blinked up at me. "I just feel tired," he said.

"Tired how?"

"Just tired." He began to curl up again, and I didn't try to stop him. If that was how he was most comfortable, then of course I'd let him be.

"Your tummy doesn't hurt?"

"No. I wanted to eat my dinner. But afterward, I felt tired."

"Then go ahead and sleep," I told him, still in that same soft, quiet voice. The last thing I wanted was for him to hear any worry in my tone, even though a nervous sensation in my gut seemed to signal this was something more than simple weariness at the end of the day. I wasn't too worried about him being sleepy at this time of night, because even though hedgehogs normally were nocturnal creatures, it seemed clear that he'd adopted the rhythms and schedule of his witch mistress. "Do you want to stay here on the rug, or would you rather come upstairs with Milo and me?"

"Upstairs," Lionel replied, the word nothing more than a breathy little whisper.

I carefully scooped him up in both hands, then climbed the stairs one by one so I wouldn't jostle him too much, my faithful cocker spaniel at my heels. It didn't seem safe to just deposit Lionel on the bed—I worried that I might roll over in the night and squish him—so I fetched a basket from the bathroom that I used to store spare washcloths, got out a fresh pillowcase and a throw blanket and used them to line the basket, and then laid the hedgehog inside before setting the basket on my bedside table. He didn't stir, but I could tell he breathed deeply and evenly.

Just sleeping, I told myself. *That's all.*

Milo had watched me carefully through all this, and then climbed onto the foot of the bed once he'd judged that the hedgehog seemed to be safely settled for the night. "Do you think he's okay?"

"He seems all right for now," I said. "And he's right here next to where we'll be sleeping, so we can keep an eye on him through the night."

Those words seemed to reassure Milo, but inside, I was still worried. There was no reason at all for Lionel to be so listless, and yet....

Oh, there's a reason, I thought grimly. *He's been hexed. Just because it didn't seem to have any effect on him earlier doesn't mean it might not be finally getting to him now.*

Question was, what could I possibly do about it?

I'd been avoiding getting in touch with Sela, and yet it didn't seem as if I had many other options. It was pretty clear she'd dumped her familiar on me because she knew about the hex and didn't want it getting in the way of her wedding trip, but these were special circumstances.

She needed to get back here and deal with the problem.

Because of my worries about Lionel, I hadn't stayed too late at Noah's house, and had left at about a quarter to ten. Now it was ten-fifteen, a time when I normally would never call someone, especially a witch I hardly knew. These were extenuating circumstances, though.

Besides, I reassured myself as I reached for my phone, *Cancun is an hour behind Salem. It's only nine-fifteen there.*

Nine-fifteen on a Saturday night. I had to imagine Sela and her new husband were out dancing the night away somewhere...or maybe doing the horizontal tango in their hotel room.

Well, no matter what she was up to, she was about to get interrupted.

I went to my contacts list and pressed the phone icon on Sela's entry. Her phone rang three times...and then went straight to voicemail.

Hi, this is Sela. I'm busy doing something fun and exciting, but if you leave your name and number, I'll call you back when I have a chance.

In other words, whenever she felt like it...which right now could be a very long time.

Fighting an overwhelming sense of futility, I went ahead and recorded a message, anyway.

"Hi, Sela. This is Charity. I discovered the hex on Lionel and tried to remove it. That didn't work, so my coven helped me out with a protection spell. It seems to be working, but now Lionel isn't doing very well. I really think you need to come back and help me figure out who could have done this to him so we can get rid of the hex. Thanks!"

That final "thanks!" sounded way too chirpy and upbeat in contrast to the content of the message I'd just left, but there wasn't much I could do about that right now. I'd only have to hope that Sela would understand how pressing the situation was and would hop on the next flight to Boston.

Wishful thinking, probably, but it was all I had right now.

After checking that Lionel was still sleeping peacefully in his basket, I went into the bathroom, performed all my usual nighttime rituals of brushing and flossing, cleansing and moisturizing, and then headed straight for my bed. Milo already appeared to be fast asleep, and I hoped I'd soon follow him into dreamland.

If nothing else, I had a feeling I'd need to be as rested as possible for whatever might come next.

Chapter 5

All the Marbles

Unfortunately, I didn't sleep as well as I'd hoped, mostly because I kept rolling over to check and make sure I hadn't missed any calls from Sela. My phone remained stubbornly silent all night, though, telling me that either she wasn't bothering to check her own phone or...even worse...she'd gotten my message but simply didn't want to deal with the problem. While there were witches here and there who eschewed all modern conveniences, most of us were all too happy to have cell phones and computers and the rest of it, so this kind of behavior definitely wasn't normal.

At least Lionel seemed to be a little better when he stretched and sat up in his basket, blinking at his unfamiliar surroundings with bright black eyes.

"Thank you for bringing me up here," he said

in his squeaky little voice. "I think I slept better than I would have downstairs."

"Well, it just made sense to have us all together," I responded, glad that he seemed to have a bit more energy this morning. "Do you think you're okay with going downstairs with Milo and me and having some breakfast?"

The hedgehog nodded, so I got out of bed, pulled on a robe and some flip-flops, then picked up Lionel's basket and carried him down to the kitchen. Milo followed closely behind and did his normal morning thing of watching me scoop his breakfast into his bowl before he headed out through the doggy door so he could take care of that morning's business.

"Do you want to go out, too?" I asked Lionel. I'd read that hedgehogs could be trained to use litter boxes, but it appeared he was much happier simply going outside like Milo did.

"Yes," said Lionel, "but I think it would be better if you carried me out there."

I told him that wasn't a problem at all, and went out the kitchen door and walked over to the oak tree so I could set him down there. "Just tell Milo when you want to come back in, and I'll come and get you."

Lionel seemed agreeable to that plan, and slowly lumbered to the other side of the oak tree where he could take care of things in private. Since hedgehogs weren't exactly known to be speed demons, it was hard to tell whether he was proceeding more deliberately than usual, or whether that was his normal gait.

But at least he was moving unassisted, so I reassured myself that he seemed to be okay for now... and that meant I could put some coffee together and try to figure out what my next step should be.

The coven's attempt to remove the hex had been a disaster, but that didn't mean I was going to throw my hands up in the air and quit. Maybe Sela would get back to me, and maybe she wouldn't. In the meantime, I had to come up with a plan of action.

Scrying had helped me with the two other murders I'd stumbled across in the past month, so I hoped maybe it would assist me now as well.

Coffee first, though. I needed a clear head.

Milo came through the back door just as I was pouring hot water into my Nespresso. "Everything okay out there?"

He nodded, even as he headed over to his bowl so he could slurp up some water. "Lionel wanted to lie in the sun for a while. But he said you could go out in a few minutes to get him."

That would give me enough time for the coffee to brew and have it cool down a bit. Then I could bring the hedgehog inside and get my morning infusion of caffeine while I came up with a plan of action.

"Did he look okay?" I asked. If Lionel hadn't, then I assumed Milo would have already let me know, but I wanted to make sure.

"He seemed fine," Milo replied. "I asked him how he was feeling, and he said better than last night. So it seemed okay for me to leave him outside a little bit longer."

That was about all I could ask for, so I let it go while I focused on my coffee prep. Soon enough, though, I was going back outside and heading over to the oak tree, where I spied Lionel's grayish, rounded form snugged up against a big tree root.

"How're you doing?" I asked, and he rolled over and squinted up at me.

"Fine," he said, then paused. "But I think I could have some breakfast now."

"Coming right up."

I carried him inside, poured some food into his bowl, and then got busy getting myself some coffee. A little dollop of cream and an even smaller bit of sugar, and then it was ready to go.

A few sips seemed to improve my outlook on life—or maybe it was just the sight of Lionel happily eating his kitty kibble that made me think things looked a lot better this morning than they had the night before. Maybe my panicked call to Sela Warren had been premature.

But no, she needed to know what was going on, at the very least, and it still seemed awfully irresponsible of her to not even call me back, even if all she planned to do was reassure me everything was fine and that I was being a drama queen.

All right, I needed to perform a scrying. Unfortunately, the next full moon wouldn't be for another week or so, and I'd used up all my moon water early in the month. Well, I'd just have to dig into my supply of distilled water and hope for the best. It had worked in the past, so I had to hope it would do the trick now, too.

Noah and I hadn't made any concrete plans for today—he knew Sunday was laundry day at my house—and that meant I should have an uninterrupted stretch of time to work on my scrying and see if I could dig up any information that might lead me back to the person who'd cast the hex on Lionel. After my coffee, I had an English muffin with some of Valerie Monroe's wonderful blackberry preserves, showered and got dressed, then came back downstairs, ready to get started.

I'd moved Lionel's basket out to the living room, since he'd told me he wanted to sleep there this morning, and Milo was with him, keeping watch even though the hedgehog seemed much improved today. But I was fine with that, because with the two familiars out in the other room, I'd have the kitchen to myself and would be better able to concentrate.

Down came the silver bowl I always used for this kind of magic from its special place in the cupboard. I set it on the kitchen table, fetched the jug of distilled water from the pantry, and slowly poured in the water, doing my best to keep it from splashing. Not because I cared about the surface of the worn table, which had suffered its share of scratches and blemishes over the years, but because I would have to wait for the water to become utterly still before I could start my magic working, and I was eager to get going.

All was quiet in the living room, telling me both the familiars were probably taking a nice mid-morning nap. Perfect.

I stood in front of the silver bowl and stared down into the clear water, doing my best to clear my mind of everything except the need to discover who had cast that awful hex on Lionel.

Mystic winds, reveal the one,
    Hex on hedgehog, evil done.
    Unmask the caster, dark or bright,
    In shadows or in broad daylight.

For the longest moment, nothing happened. Then, very slowly, billowy gray clouds appeared to form in the water.

Nothing else, though. Was this some kind of other interference from the witch who'd cast the spell, something that blocked my scrying in the same way the coven's spell had been deflected on Friday night?

Maybe. I'd never encountered anything like this before, so it was hard for me to say for sure.

Well, I'd already sworn that I wasn't going to give up, so a small roadblock like this wasn't enough to make me put away the scrying bowl.

Time for a different spell.

Hedgehog's quill, so sharp and bright,
Reveal the caster, hidden from sight,
With this spell, their name take flight,
Unmask the hexer in mystic light.

If anything, the clouds on the surface of the water only increased in size and density. Obviously, I was going about this the wrong way.

Problem was, I didn't know what the right way was supposed to be.

Okay, maybe rather than trying to go directly to the source—in other words, the witch who had cast the spell—I should try to re-create Lionel's

surroundings when it happened. I had to believe
he'd been hit with the curse fairly recently, or Sela
wouldn't have been in any shape to pack her bags
and head for Mexico. No, she would have fallen
down the stairs or been in a broomstick accident,
something that would have kept her close to home.

Home. That was where I needed to start. Not
my house, of course, but Sela's place in Marblehead. Since I already knew what I was dealing with,
this shouldn't be too difficult.

Spirit's whisper, secrets unveil,
   Show me where Sela's home does dwell.

To my utter relief, the heavy gray clouds that
had been obscuring the surface of the mirror parted
at last, showing me what looked like the living
room of a house that appeared to be around the
same vintage as mine, probably built sometime in
the early nineteenth century. Unlike my house,
though, hers had been updated to a stylish California coastal vibe that didn't quite match the
home's structural details but still managed to be
charming.

Only....

My stomach clenched as I squinted down at
the surface of the mirror. Was that someone's foot
sticking out from behind the beige linen sectional?

Scrying wasn't like dropping a video camera

into someone's house; you couldn't exactly give it commands to pan around and try to capture images from a different angle. Still, this was magic we were dealing with, so I wasn't powerless, either.

Turn the axis, shift the view,
Reveal this room from angles new,
With mystic power, I now decree,
Show the unseen, let visions be.

A gasp escaped my lips. Yes, a dark-haired, slender woman was lying, apparently lifeless, on the white oak floor directly behind the sectional, her still face staring up at the ceiling. For one awful minute, I thought it was Sela herself, since she looked so similar, but then I realized this woman was probably a couple of years older, her hair a little longer, a little wavier.

Her sister?

Sela hadn't mentioned a sister, but that didn't mean much. It wasn't as if we'd exchanged life stories when she dropped off Lionel—no, she'd been in a hell of a hurry to get out of Salem, and hadn't given me anything other than a quick explanation of her itinerary, not even bothering to spell out the details of her familiar's care and feeding. Clearly, she'd thought I'd be able to figure it out on my own.

How long had the woman been lying there in

Sela's living room? Her face was ghost pale, her eyelids somehow sunken and bruised, telling me she must have been dead for at least a couple of hours, if not even longer than that. I was no expert, so that was a hasty guess and nothing more.

Derek Falco would know went through my mind, and I batted the thought aside as quickly as it had come. Like the situation wasn't complicated enough already.

This wasn't his jurisdiction, though—Sela Warren lived in Marblehead, so this would be a problem for the Marblehead police department, not ours.

I knew I had to make that call. First, though, I needed to gather the coven once again.

"That's definitely Anna Warren," Tonya Willis said as she gazed down into the scrying bowl, and I stared at my fellow coven mate in surprise.

"You know her?"

"Yes," Tonya said. Although she sounded calm enough, I could tell by the tension in her jaw and the way she pressed her lips together that seeing the other woman's dead body in the calm waters of the silvery bowl had upset her more than she wanted to let on. "I was born in Marblehead, although my family moved to Salem when I was in high school."

I hadn't known that. Then again, Tonya was more of my mother's generation than mine, so it wasn't as though we hung out together. She was a member of the coven, someone whose presence I took for granted because she'd been a part of my life pretty much from the day I was born. Not exactly a type of aunt, I supposed, since she was so busy that she'd rarely attended my birthday parties or graduations when I was growing up, but someone who always gave me a gift at Yule and who had occasionally watched me when my mother had a doctor's appointment or some other reason why she couldn't be there for me after I got home from school.

"Anyway," she went on, "I keep in touch with some of the witches in Marblehead, and I knew Sela's mother. She passed away a couple of years ago—cancer, I think."

Despite Sela's continuing radio silence, I couldn't help but feel a stab of pity for her. She was too young to have lost her mother...and now her sister was gone as well.

"We have to call the police," Grace said, and Tonya's mouth tightened further.

"Yes," she agreed, her tone clearly reluctant, "but first, I need to go to Sela's house and see if I can determine whether magic was involved or whether she died of natural causes—a sudden stroke, maybe, or a fall. It's hard to tell just from looking in the scrying mirror, but it's possible she might have tripped on something and hit her head."

That scenario didn't seem very plausible to me. However, I was forced to admit that it was possible Anna Warren had a nasty bump on the side of her head we couldn't see. The only way to know for sure was to go there in person.

"Take Charity with you," my mother suggested, and both Tonya and I blinked at her in surprise.

"Why?" Tonya asked, and then sent me an apologetic look. "No offense, Charity, but I'm not sure what you can do to help."

"She's already solved two murders," my mother told her. "I think she's the best one of our coven to go with you. The two of you can do a quick reconnaissance, and then you can call the Marblehead police."

For a moment, Tonya didn't say anything. I wasn't sure whether I should try to protest that I was no homicide detective and didn't know how much help I would be, but I kept quiet. If nothing else, going with Tonya to Sela's house might provide me with a few more clues to help solve the puzzle of Lionel's hex.

"All right," Tonya said at last. "We'll have to make it quick, though. We don't want to attract any unnecessary attention."

I had a feeling we were going to attract plenty of attention once we called the Marblehead police, but first things first. We absolutely had to know whether any magical foul play had been involved in Anna's death, because it wasn't anything we wanted the police to discover on their own. Most spells didn't leave any traces, and yet there was enough of a chance that something might look fishy to the authorities that we needed to know if any quick obfuscation might be required.

Using broomsticks in broad daylight was always risky. Instead, Tonya and I drove to Sela's house—which was only about fifteen minutes away—in Tonya's Mercedes. I always considered it kind of a flashy car for a witch to own, but since she was a very successful real estate agent, I supposed it was something her clients would expect her to have.

And I had to admit it was pure luxury after bouncing around in my Discovery, with its quarter-million miles.

Sela's house turned out to be a darling two-story cottage, dark blue with white trim and a cheerful red door, and red geraniums blooming on the front porch.

Or at least, the house would have looked cheerful if I hadn't known what was waiting for us behind that red door.

On the drive over, Tonya and I had already

decided we would use as much of the truth as possible in the story we gave the police. I was watching Sela's pet hedgehog while she was on her wedding trip to Cancun, and we'd come over to the house to get more of his food when the supply Sela had given me was running low. None of that sounded too out of the ordinary, and the little white lie gave us a reason for coming here in the first place.

She hadn't given me a key, but that didn't matter. Not when witches were involved.

Tonya murmured a door-unlocking spell, and the two of us stepped inside. I'd halfway been expecting to be greeted by some kind of horrible odor from the body that lay somewhere farther into the house, but obviously, Anna hadn't been dead long enough for that to be a problem.

No, all I could detect was a faint herbal scent that probably came from a bowl of pot-pourri somewhere, and maybe the faintest aroma of beeswax furniture polish.

While I hesitated in the tiny foyer, Tonya went ahead and walked into the living room.

"Yes, she's here," she said.

Only a few weeks ago, I'd had to confront a dead body in the living room of the Airbnb Shelby Howard had been renting, and I had no real desire to repeat the experience. But because this was the entire reason why Tonya and I had come here, I knew I couldn't hang back, even though my heart beat faster than I would have liked and I couldn't ignore the slightly sick sensation in my stomach.

Just as I'd seen in the scrying mirror, Sela's sister lay on the wood floor behind the big beige sectional. Mercifully, her eyes were shut, and from where I stood, I couldn't see a mark on her.

Tonya murmured another spell under her breath, most likely one to let her know whether someone had hexed poor Anna as well, or whether the woman really had passed away from natural causes, as unlikely as that particular scenario seemed.

"Well?" I asked, after a few seconds had gone by and Tonya still hadn't said anything.

She released a breath. "It was definitely magic," she said. "Dark magic, the kind that will make the mundies think she died of a stroke. But I can sense the stink of the magic used here."

Cold worked its way down my spine. I couldn't help thinking of Brian Alatorre, who'd been dispatched by means of a similar spell. His had been pretty much a mercy killing, though, while I couldn't think of any plausible reason why someone would want a harmless-looking witch like Anna Warren out of the way.

"What do we do now?" I asked. Although I

was a grown woman of nearly thirty, I still couldn't help feeling relieved that Tonya was there with me. Tonya was twice my age, with much more life experience, and it just seemed natural to look to her for guidance in this extremely difficult situation.

Her lips compressed again. "We call the police."

Chapter 6

Ripples from the Splash

"And how did you know Anna Warren?" the Marblehead P.D. detective, Chuck Finley, asked Tonya. He was nowhere near as striking as Derek Falco, being only an inch or two taller than I, with balding fair hair and a paunch that his belt barely managed to keep in check.

But then, it didn't really matter what he looked like as long as he was good at his job.

"Anna's and my families have known each other for years," Tonya said calmly. "I was born here in Marblehead and didn't move away until I was in high school." She looked a little shaky as she spoke, but mostly composed. That was probably easier to accomplish now, since several EMTs had already taken away Anna's body, presumably to the local medical examiner's office.

"And you were looking after the victim's sister's pet?" Detective Finley inquired next, now looking over at me.

"Yes," I said. "But she was in a hurry and hadn't brought enough food for Lionel, so I came over here to get some more."

"You had a key?"

"Yes," I lied, even as I hoped he wouldn't ask me to produce one. Tonya had used a door-unlocking spell to get into the house, so I knew there wouldn't be any sign of forced entry. Still, without a key, it would be difficult to explain how we'd gotten in.

Luckily, the detective didn't press me on that issue. "Any reason why the two of you came here together?"

Suspicious type, wasn't he? To my relief, a ready lie bubbled to my lips.

"My car's in the shop. I mentioned to Tonya that I needed to come to Marblehead, and she said she'd drive me."

True, I could have taken the bus—Marblehead was only a few miles away from Salem, although it would've been a hefty walk for me to get from my home on Winter Island Drive to the nearest bus stop—but my story must have seemed plausible enough to Detective Finley, because he only nodded.

"All right," he said. "So, you entered the house

and found Ms. Warren's body."

"Yes," I replied. "She was lying behind the sectional."

I pointed, probably an unnecessary gesture, since the detective had already inspected the place where Anna had fallen.

"Any sign that anyone else had been here?"

"No," Tonya said crisply. "Nothing seemed to have been disturbed, and the door was locked when we got here."

Another very brief nod, since what we were both saying corroborated what he already knew. "Any theories as to why Anna Warren would have been in her sister's house?"

"We just assumed she must have been keeping an eye on things while Sela was out of the country," Tonya replied. "Sela has a lot of plants that need watering."

Which was true. The pair of fiddle-leaf figs in the living room were real, not silk, and ivy and philodendron cascaded from the bookshelves. And although I hadn't gone into the kitchen, even from where I stood, I could spy a window box filled with flowers and herbs.

The detective made a few notes, then closed the little yellow pad he held. "Well, I think that's about it," he said. "All signs point to death from natural causes, but we'll wait for the medical examiner to provide that information. If I have any other questions, I'll be in touch."

"What about the plants?" I blurted. As someone who cultivated her own herb garden—albeit one outside in the garden, not in a window box—I couldn't help worrying about what would happen to the lovely specimens in Sela's home.

"I'll let you know when you can come back in," Detective Finley told me. "But until you hear otherwise, this is an active crime scene, and you'll need to stay away."

Because even though the detective seemed to think that Anna had died of a stroke or something similar, he still had several detectives, their hands swathed in plastic gloves, gathering what I assumed were stray pieces of hair and anything else they thought might help to determine what had really happened to her.

Had Anna's killer left behind some kind of evidence?

As soon as that thought passed through my mind, however, I had to dismiss it. The kind of magic that had killed Anna Warren wasn't the sort of thing you needed to deploy at point-blank range. No, the witch who'd cast that spell had probably been miles away, safe in the knowledge that no regular detective or police force or even the FBI and its advanced labs could ever discover what she'd done.

Which meant it was up to me and the members of my coven to discover the truth. Thank God that at least on this one, I wouldn't have to go it alone.

"That's not a problem," Tonya told Detective Finley. "Charity will keep on watching Lionel until she hears from Sela."

Now the detective frowned. "We haven't been able to get hold of Ms. Warren yet. Have you spoken to her recently?"

"No," I said. "I tried to call her last night—you know, to check in and let her know how things were going with Lionel—but she never picked up."

"Same here," Detective Finley said. "Went to voicemail."

"Well, she went to Cancun to get married," Tonya reminded him. "She's probably not checking her phone very often."

And what a horrible surprise she would get once she finally did think to listen to her messages. I twinged inwardly, imagining how awful it would be to get some of the worst news ever, right while you were off trying to celebrate a new and happy stage in your life.

I didn't know any of the Marblehead witches very well, but I hoped they'd be able to offer Sela the support she would need once she got back home. True, she had a husband who should also be there for her, and yet he wouldn't have been a part of her life for nearly as long as the witches she'd grown up with, who were a part of her coven.

Detective Finley's expression was grim. "Here's hoping she checks in sooner rather than later. But you ladies can get on with your Sunday now."

His words were a mostly polite way of phrasing it, but clearly, he thought we'd provided all the useful information we could, and now he needed us out of the way. Which was fine. I wanted to get far, far away from that cute little house with its stink of death and dark magic. No, it wasn't an actual smell, nothing the human nose could detect, but now that I knew what had happened here, all my witch senses were telling me I needed to leave.

And we did, after telling the detective we'd be in contact if we could think of anything else. In grim silence, we headed over to Tonya's Mercedes S-Class, then buckled ourselves in. A few minutes later, we were out on Highway 114, driving just a couple of miles above the speed limit as she pointed the big, shiny car toward Salem.

"This is just terrible," Tonya said a moment later, breaking the unsettled quiet. "I keep thinking of Sela down there in Cancun, having the time of her life, never realizing...."

The words trailed off there, but I knew exactly what she meant. Everything in Sela's life would be forever divided between the time when she believed her sister was alive, and the terrible moment afterward when she realized Anna had been taken from her in such a horrible way.

"Well, once she gets back in contact, we'll have to let her know that the Salem witch community is here for her if she needs us," I replied, and Tonya tilted her head slightly.

"I'm sure the Marblehead witches will rally around her," she said. "But right now, the more important thing is for us to try to find out who could have done this to Anna, and why. I didn't know her well, but from what I've heard, she didn't seem like the sort of person who would attract this kind of dark magic. She wasn't the sort of witch that another magic-worker could have possibly perceived as a threat."

"Maybe it was some kind of private feud?" I suggested, even though I honestly couldn't think of a reason for one witch to turn on another in this kind of way. When I'd first discovered the hex on Lionel, Sage and I had speculated maybe it had been cast because Sela had taken off with another witch's lover and that was why she'd left the country so quickly, but that didn't seem to be the driving force behind what had happened to Anna.

Or...was it?

"Do you know if Anna was married?" I asked before Tonya could respond to my first question.

"No. Like many of us, she was single." Maybe the faintest of smiles...was Tonya thinking of my burgeoning relationship with Noah Jenkins?... before she went on, "Happily so, from what I'd heard. So I doubt we're dealing with a jealous rival here or anything like that."

That probably would have made things too easy. "Well, I guess we'll have to start looking into her life, her activities, so we can see if anything jumps out at us."

Tonya sent me a sideways glance before returning her attention to the road. "I'm not sure that's a very good idea."

I blinked at her, wondering what in the world had prompted her to respond that way. "Why not? I mean, why did we go over to her house in the first place if we weren't going to mount our own investigation? Detective Finley seems competent enough, but there's no way in the world he'll be able to discover that it was really magic that killed Anna Warren. That means we have to do it."

"No, it means the Marblehead witches need to mount their own investigation," Tonya replied, in a tone that didn't seem to invite much argument. "Obviously, we'll offer any help we can give if they ask for it, but just think how it would be if the situation was reversed, if one of our own passed away under suspicious circumstances and the witches from Marblehead tried to come over and stick their noses into our business."

I hadn't really thought about the situation that

way, but she had a point. In general, while witches weren't completely territorial, we tended to stay on our own home ground and not involve ourselves in the affairs of other communities unless we were expressly invited. Some of us, like Tonya, ranged farther afield because of their work—her real estate office was located in Salem, although she also sold houses in Marblehead and Swampscott and Peabody and Beverly as well—but for the most part we didn't, to use Tonya's own phrase, stick our noses in where they didn't belong.

"I suppose so," I said slowly. While I could understand her reasoning, that didn't mean I had to like it.

"And the reason we went to Sela's house was to make sure that what you saw in the scrying mirror was correct," Tonya went on. "Think how awful it would have been if Anna had only been hurt, and we'd stayed away when we could have gone there and helped her."

I hadn't even thought about that, but Tonya was right. The image in the mirror had made it look as though Anna was dead, but there had always been the chance that she'd merely been unconscious. If that had been the case, then our intervention might have meant the difference between life and death.

Tragically, she was gone long before we came on the scene, but there had been no way for us to have known that for sure without being there in person.

I made a sound of assent and figured there wasn't much reason to discuss the topic any further. Tonya had made her point, and, even though I didn't completely like it, I understood where she was coming from. If the Marblehead witches reached out and asked us to help, then we'd do whatever we could to assist them in tracking down Anna's killer.

Until then....

Well, until then, I'd take the best possible care of Lionel. At least he'd seemed improved this morning, and that was something.

But when I returned home—Tonya had told me she'd be in touch with the rest of the coven to let them know what we'd found in Marblehead—it was to find Lionel once again drooping and listless in the basket I'd procured for him, and I experienced that sinking sensation in my stomach once again.

"I don't know what happened," Milo said, furry brown forehead furrowed with worry. "One minute he was just fine, and the other, he couldn't climb into his basket. I had to pick him up with my teeth and put him there." He paused, black lips wrinkling a little. "Hedgehogs are cute, but they taste awful."

With all those spines, I could only imagine. True, Lionel wouldn't have been on the defensive, and wouldn't have made himself as spiky as he might have if he'd been trying to protect himself from a predator, but still, I guessed it hadn't been a very pleasant experience for Milo.

I patted the dog on the head and told him he was a good boy, then went into the living room so I could kneel down next to Lionel's basket, which was sitting next to the hearth where I'd left it. As Milo had said, the hedgehog was curled into a tight ball, the rise and fall of his little sides barely perceptible.

"Hey, there," I said softly. "Milo said you were feeling tired again."

Lionel barely stirred, moving just enough so I could see the side of his face as he spoke. "I am," he whispered. "I thought I was better this morning."

"Well, maybe you just overdid it a little," I replied, my tone gentle but also—I hoped—encouraging at the same time. "It's okay if you want to nap. Is there anything I can get you?"

"No," the hedgehog said. "Just want to sleep."

His little eyes closed, and he went back into a tightly curled ball, his face hidden from me. Worried, I got back to my feet and met the gaze of my equally concerned cocker spaniel.

"What's wrong with him?" Milo asked.

"I don't know," I said, knowing I sounded just as frustrated as I felt. "Maybe it's something to do with the hex, but if so, I don't know why he seemed so much better this morning."

"Maybe he only has so much energy every day, and he thought he had more than he did and used it up all at once."

Milo's suggestion made just about as much sense as anything else I could think of. I stooped to ruffle his ears and said, "That's very possible. I guess it means we need to keep an extra-close watch on him so he doesn't overdo things tomorrow morning when he thinks he's feeling a little better."

"I can do that."

We both needed to, which meant I'd have to bring both familiars with me to work the next day. I didn't want to make Milo solely responsible for watching Lionel, not when neither of us really knew what was going on.

At least Mondays tended to be quiet at the shop, since I only had Monday hours during the high season in the summer, and I should have enough free time to be able to go in the back of the store and check on the hedgehog as often as I needed to. A panicky little thought went through me.

What if, despite my best efforts, the hex got the better of him? How in the world would Sela react to losing her sister and her familiar in the space of a couple days?

It's not going to happen, I told myself firmly. *I won't let it.*

I just wished I could allow myself to believe that.

Although hanging out at the store was definitely not on Milo's list of favorite things to do—he much preferred having free rein to roam my back-yard as he wished—he dutifully got in the front seat of my Land Rover the next morning, and waited while I went back to strap in Lionel's basket in the spot that most people would have used for a car seat. The little guy was already asleep, and didn't even blink as I fastened the seatbelt with an audible *click*.

As I'd thought, the hedgehog had woken up claiming to feel much better, but I'd managed to convince him that he needed to conserve his energy, since I knew it wouldn't last. Sure enough, he got droopy after eating his breakfast, but climbed into his basket under his own power, even if he nodded off soon afterward.

In a way, that was better. While I would have preferred to see him up and around and as chipper as he'd been when Sela dropped him off, at least this way I knew he would stay put.

When Sage came in, she sent an inquiring look toward the basket, which was sitting at the end of the counter.

"I'll put him in back when we open the doors," I said. "But he's not doing very well, so I didn't want to leave him at the house."

"He's adorable," Sage replied, after taking a quick glance inside the basket. "I'll help you keep an eye on him, too. I've never had a hedgehog, but I had a hamster when I was a kid."

Which gave her way more rodent-adjacent experience than I did. Grace Bowersby had a rat familiar named Jonah, but since she and Jonah got along very well—she even took him in her purse when she went to get a manicure—I'd never had any reason to have him come stay with me. None of the other familiars I'd ever worked with had been rats or mice, so, even though a hedgehog wasn't technically a rodent, Sage probably had a better idea of what she was doing than I did.

"Thank you," I said, and hoped she could hear the gratitude in my voice.

She nodded, but then seemed to think it was time to move on to more pressing matters. "My mom told me about what happened to Anna Warren," she said in an undertone, even though we still had ten minutes before the store opened and were there alone.

"It's horrible," I agreed. "And it's even worse that I haven't heard a single thing from Sela. The detective with the Marblehead police said he hadn't been able to get hold of her, either."

"Maybe her phone died, and she forgot to bring the charger?" Sage suggested.

I supposed that explanation might have made some sense...except Sela was vacationing in Cancun, not the jungles of Borneo. Even if she'd been so hasty in packing that she'd left her phone charger behind, she still should have been able to buy a replacement in a shop somewhere.

No, this felt more like someone who was hoping if she could ignore the rest of the world, it would ignore her right back.

"I hope that's all it is," I said, and left it there. Sela hadn't even told me the name of the hotel where she was staying, so I couldn't try reaching out that way.

But I had to believe the Marblehead police had lots of resources even a witch like me didn't have access to. It was possible they'd already gotten hold of her itinerary, maybe by reaching out to the various airlines until they tracked her down.

Then again, this was a local police department we were talking about, not the FBI. They could be just as much in the dark as I was...and would remain so, unless Sela suddenly decided to break her radio silence.

Sage seemed to realize I didn't want to keep talking about the situation, especially since there wasn't much of anything I could do about it. Instead, she did her usual quick pass of the racks of dried herbs and the shelves of tinctures and elixirs, making sure everything was where it needed to be.

And then it was time to open up. At least today there wasn't a crowd of people waiting outside, the way there sometimes was on a weekend or a holiday when we'd get some early-bird busloads of tourists. No, I unlocked the door with little ceremony, then went and slipped the key into its usual compartment inside the cash register.

In fact, our first customer of the day really wasn't a customer at all.

No, that was Derek Falco who walked in a few minutes after ten. Like the first time I'd met him, he was wearing a white button-down shirt, khaki pants, and a tie, telling me he was probably here on official business...or at least, had come by when he was on duty.

"I hear you've gotten caught up in another mysterious death," he remarked, after sending a quick sideways look in Sage's direction. Since she was busy hanging up new packets of dried herbs on the large sales rack on the other side of the room, he probably figured it was safe to talk.

He also seemed to take in the presence of Lionel's basket on the countertop without even a blink, but because he'd most likely heard that I fostered a sometimes bewildering variety of animals, he seemed to decide he'd better not comment on the addition of a hedgehog to today's routine.

And thank God he'd said "mysterious death" and not "murder," which seemed to tell me the medical examiner hadn't found anything out of the ordinary about Anna's death.

Well, except that she'd been a woman in her mid-thirties in good health, and not the kind of person who usually dropped dead out of the blue.

"It's awful," I said, which I thought was a safe enough reply. "Especially since no one has been able to get hold of Anna's sister."

Derek nodded, again seeming to indicate that he'd heard at least some particulars of the case. Maybe he had friends in the Marblehead force, or maybe the various local police departments had their own version of a witchy grapevine.

"Yeah, Chuck isn't too happy about that," Derek remarked. "It's like she vanished into thin air."

"I thought she was in Cancun," I said, startled. "I mean, that's what Sela told me when she dropped off Lionel."

And I inclined my head toward the hedgehog, still asleep in his basket.

Derek rubbed a contemplative thumb over his

chin. "Not that Chuck has been able to determine. There's no record of Sela Warren leaving on any outbound flights from Boston, and no one by that name staying in any hotels in Cancun."

Well, there was something I hadn't been expecting. It really did sound as though Sela had disappeared into thin air.

Did she intend to leave Lionel with me forever?

No, a witch would never do something like that. Or at least, I didn't want to think she would. Up until the time Darla Fitzgerald had crossed my path a few weeks ago, I'd believed the connection between a witch and her familiar was sacrosanct, that even if they might be experiencing some temporary difficulties, she would never, ever abandon her animal companion.

But Darla's connection to Milo had been tenuous enough that he'd managed to survive despite her untimely death, and the reality of that situation had been enough of a blow that I realized I needed to reexamine some of my assumptions. For all I knew, Sela had convinced herself Lionel would be safe with me precisely because I'd taken in Milo and given him a home.

However, while she'd seemed distracted, she hadn't seemed cold or distant the way Darla had been when she first dropped Milo off at my house. No, Sela had almost seemed...scared?

Scared of what? The same witch who'd murdered her sister?

I pushed the thought aside for further examination later. Hoping Derek hadn't seen any of my inner conflict or worry in my face, I said, "Well, maybe she was using a different name. She did go to Cancun to get married, after all."

Now he smiled a little, as if amused by my lack of subject knowledge in that particular arena. "That process takes at least two weeks after the wedding, most times a lot longer," he told me. "No, she would've had the tickets listed under her maiden name, even if she planned to change it after she got back from her honeymoon."

Well, there went that idea. "What does Detective Finley think?"

Derek's smile disappeared. "He doesn't know what to think. Neither does anyone else—at least, not yet. But it does seem kind of suspicious, although it looks as though Anna Warren died of natural causes."

"She did?" I said, knowing those two syllables came out sounding way too hopeful. "I mean," I went on quickly, "that's what Tonya and I thought must have happened, but we couldn't figure out how someone that young—"

"Cerebral aneurysm," Derek broke in, but gently. "It's rare but not unheard-of. I doubt Anna had any idea anything was wrong."

Well, that was something, I supposed. I hoped the day of my own demise was far, far off in the future, but when it happened, better to go like that —no warning, nothing to make you think anything was different about this particular moment from all the thousands of other moments that had already preceded it.

True, that aneurysm had been caused by some very dark magic and not an accident of biology, but still, I supposed it could have been a lot worse.

"No, it's this thing with Sela that seems to be the real mystery," Derek went on. "It sounds like Chuck is trying to see if he can track down anyone related to this 'Colin' who was supposedly Sela's fiancé, but so far, none of her friends even seem to know his last name. She only referred to him by his first name and never mentioned his profession."

Stranger and stranger. Then again, what I knew —and Derek and the Marblehead P.D. didn't—was that Sela would have faced some stiff opposition in the witch community for getting so serious with someone after only knowing him for a month. She might have been consciously vague in an attempt to protect him.

As soon as I entertained that thought, I wanted to laugh at myself. Yes, she probably would have been on the receiving end of a few lectures— including a couple from her sister—but disapproving witches didn't exactly constitute a physical threat.

Only...what if they did? What if the Marblehead witches were angry enough with Sela for being so careless that they were willing to do whatever it took in order to ensure their true identities remained a secret?

"Did you think of something?" Derek asked, and I blinked.

"What?"

"You looked as though you just had a flash of inspiration."

Well, so much for my poker face. "Oh, nothing," I said hastily. "I suppose I was just thinking it was too bad Sela never mentioned what Colin did for a living, because the Marblehead police might have had an easier time trying to figure out his identity."

"It does seem as if she kept her cards pretty close to the vest when it came to talking about who he was," Derek commented. "Not even her business partner—she owns half a company that supplies live plants to local businesses and restaurants—seems to know anything about him."

Well, that explained why all the plants in Sela's house looked so gorgeous, so luxuriant. Was her business partner another witch, or an unaware mundie who had no idea Sela was a little bit more than just a woman with a green thumb?

So much I needed to find out. Right then, I didn't care that Tonya had said I needed to stay out of this and let the Marblehead witches handle a matter that had involved one of their own. If they'd disapproved of Sela's relationship with Colin, then maybe they wouldn't work too hard to figure out where she'd gone...or who had killed her sister.

Especially if it had been one of them all along.

"It does seem like a real mystery," I agreed. "And obviously, I'll contact Detective Finley right away if Sela ever calls me back."

"I figured you would." A pause, one during which Derek's expression shifted subtly, as though he wanted to say something else...something that had absolutely nothing to do with Sela or Anna Warren...and then thought better of it. "Well, I'll let you get back to work."

"Thanks for filling me in on what's happening with Anna's case," I replied, since I wasn't quite sure what else to say. Odd emotions seemed to war within me. Was I disappointed that he hadn't tried to ask me out again?

No, that was crazy.

"I figured I owed you one after you helped me out with that whole mess with the Millers," Derek said easily. "Have a good day."

And then he headed out the door as Sage finally emerged from the racks of dried herbs.

"He's hot," she said.

Not helping, I thought. Out loud, I only responded, "He's probably at least twelve years older than you are."

"So? Ryan Gosling's even older than that, and I still think he's hot."

"Detective Falco just wanted to talk to me about the Warren sisters," I said, although my protest sounded a little weak even to me.

Sage shot me the kind of side-eye that only a twenty-two-year-old could muster. "Keep telling yourself that," she remarked, then leaned down to peek into Lionel's basket before she picked up the feather duster we kept under the counter and headed over to the small display of handcrafted teapots I kept at the back of the store. "I saw the way he was looking at you."

I considered several different retorts, decided they were all kind of weak, and instead pretended to be occupied with counting out the change in the cash register, something I'd done before Sage had even gotten here. Still, she didn't have to know that.

How *had* Derek been looking at me? I honestly couldn't say for sure, because I'd been too preoccupied during our conversation to be worried about anything so mundane.

Well, mostly. Maybe his gaze had been kind of admiring. That didn't matter, though, because I was with Noah, and also, I had far more important things to occupy my brain.

No matter what else was going on, it definitely sounded as though I needed to embark on the kind of the investigation the Marblehead P.D. would never be able to undertake.

Chapter 7

Planting a Seed

SOME QUICK GOOGLING DURING MY LUNCH break told me that the company Sela and her business partner owned was called Leaf and Flower, and they had a storefront on Washington Street in Marblehead. Sela's co-owner was someone named Maggie Phillips. Her photo on the company's "About" page showed a woman who looked like she was in her early forties, with no-nonsense short-cropped blonde hair and features that were friendly rather than beautiful.

I had to wonder how the two of them had even met, since there was enough of an age gap that they wouldn't have been school friends or anything like that. But small towns offered plenty of chances to meet kindred spirits, and I supposed their paths might have crossed at a plant show or something like that.

The important thing was that the company actually had a storefront, making it easier for me to go meet Maggie in person. On the website, it said "By Appointment Only," though, which meant I had to call first and pretend as though I wanted to turn Full Moon Apothecary into some kind of tropical paradise.

When Maggie answered the phone, she sounded worried...which I supposed wasn't all that strange, considering her business partner's sister had just been found dead the day before. "Leaf and Flower, this is Maggie."

"Hi, Maggie," I said. "My name's Charity Hughes, and I own a shop in Salem on Essex Street. I've been trying to give it a little makeover, and someone suggested your business to me. Do you service the Salem area?"

"Oh, yes," Maggie replied at once. "We cover a twenty-five-mile radius, and you're well within that. Do you want to schedule an appointment so I can come look at your space?"

I hadn't been expecting that kind of offer. Somehow, I'd just thought I'd go to her office and discuss my plant needs with her there.

Correctly interpreting the silence that followed her question, she said, "It really helps if I can come take a look at the space where the plants are going. Then I can analyze the available light, see how much room you have, that kind of thing. Sometimes it can get a little complicated."

I supposed so. And actually, having her come to Full Moon Apothecary would be fine...if she was okay with waiting until after we'd closed. "Can you come after five, like maybe five-fifteen?" I asked. "We close at five o'clock. I just figured it would be easier to have you look at the store without tripping over a bunch of customers."

A small chuckle came through my iPhone's speaker. "I can do that," Maggie assured me. "A lot of my consults are after hours. Can I have your address?"

I gave it to her, even as I reflected that this was going to work out a lot better than my original plan. Now I wouldn't have to leave Sage to keep an eye on the store—and Lionel and Milo—while I went chasing over to Marblehead. Both the animals had been very quiet all day...Lionel because he was sleeping the whole time, and Milo because he was such a good dog, even though I knew he must be bored and would rather have been at home, where he could come and go through the doggy door as he pleased. Sage had offered to walk him on her lunch break, and that had perked him up a little. Still, I knew it would be asking a lot of her to babysit both animals while I drove over to the next town, so this was a much more convenient solution.

However, I didn't say anything to my assistant about my plans. For one thing, I had no idea whether Maggie Phillips would even have any useful information to offer, and since we were dealing with a witch—or witches—who didn't have a problem with casting death spells and hexing innocent little creatures, I figured the less Sage knew, the better.

So I acted as if this was just a regular day, and since I often lingered to get everything buttoned up after she'd left, she didn't seem to suspect anything was strange about this particular Monday afternoon. No, she only said goodbye, and that she hoped Lionel would be feeling better tomorrow, then headed out back to where her Nissan Leaf was parked.

Milo sent me an inquisitive glance when it became obvious that I didn't plan to follow her anytime soon. "Aren't we going home?"

There might have been the slightest hint of a whine in his voice. Eight-plus hours was an awfully long time for him to have been cooped up in the store—lunch-hour walks notwithstanding—and I bent down so I could scratch him behind the ears.

"I'm sorry, Milo," I said. "I have someone meeting me here in a couple of minutes. But we'll go home after that."

Because he was an awfully smart dog, he asked, "Is it something to do with Lionel's mistress?"

"Yes," I replied. "I'm meeting her sister's business partner."

He knew all about Anna's death, and his expression sobered. "Oh. I understand. I'll just go wait in my bed."

And he headed toward the back of the shop, where I'd set up a dog bed and his food bowls behind a folding Japanese screen a while back. A peek inside Lionel's basket told me he was still sleeping. I placed a gentle hand on him, letting myself feel the way his tiny sides rose and fell.

Still alive, thank God. For how long, though?

I didn't want to imagine such a thing, but since he hadn't shown any signs of improvement today, I wasn't sure what to think.

Then again, maybe this was the worst the hex had in store for him. It was sad to see him curled up in that basket for hours and hours, sleeping his life away, but on the other hand, it was still better than the alternative.

A knock on the shop door made me look up from Lionel's basket. I'd locked the door at five, just like I always did, which meant I had to hurry over to let Maggie Phillips in.

She was shorter in person than I'd expected, but practically radiated energy nonetheless. "Hi," she said. "I'm Maggie Phillips."

And she extended a hand.

I shook it, noting her firm grip, then said, "And

I'm Charity Hughes. Thanks so much for coming out here on such short notice."

"It's fine," she replied. "Gave me something else to focus on."

Because I couldn't pretend not to know what had happened to Anna Warren—not when I'd invited Maggie here expressly to find out anything I could about Sela and the mysterious Colin—I gave a sober nod. "I heard about Anna Warren."

Maggie didn't ask me how I knew. Her gaze moved past me to Lionel's basket, and she said, "You're the gal who was watching Sela's hedgehog."

I nodded. "Yes, I do a lot of animal fostering, so I suppose that's why Sela came to me to look after Lionel while she was out of the country." I paused, then decided I might as well go for it. "Have you heard anything from her?"

For a second or two, Maggie didn't reply. After giving me a very shrewd look, she said, "You don't really need plants for your shop, do you?"

I'd actually been pondering that question before she even arrived, and had come to the conclusion that the store could use a little sprucing up...so to speak. "I actually am interested in doing something here," I said. "But maybe we could talk about Sela first."

Maggie ran a hand through her short-cropped blonde hair. Some silver glinted among the honey-colored strands, making me think maybe she was older than she looked at first glance...or was going prematurely gray and wasn't worried about trying to cover it up.

"She had an amazing gift with plants," she said. "We met about six years ago. My business was really taking off, and I needed an assistant."

I blinked. "I thought she was your business partner."

"Oh, she is now," Maggie replied. "A couple of years ago, she wanted to invest some of her inheritance in the business, so we moved to our current storefront, and she became a fifty-percent owner of Leaf and Flower."

That made sense. A lot of witches tended to be independent business owners, just because it was easier to keep the magical part of our lives secret when we weren't dealing with an office full of co-workers. That Sela had gone into business with a mundie was a little surprising, though; working that closely with someone who could never learn anything about her witch nature had to have been difficult for her.

Obviously, I couldn't comment on any of that. No, I only said, "Ah, okay. That makes sense."

"But I haven't heard anything from her, if that's why you wanted to talk to me," Maggie said, again being just a little too shrewd about my motivations. "The day before she left, she told me she'd be back on the twenty-sixth, and that was the last time I heard from her."

"But she was definitely planning to come back."

That comment earned me a startled blink. "Of course she was planning to come back," Maggie replied, her tone emphatic. "She has a business and a life here—and a new husband to be a part of that life."

"Did you ever meet Colin?" I asked next, deciding I might as well go for it. True, Derek had told me that Sela's business partner didn't know much about the man who was her fiancé, but maybe Maggie had been holding back for Sela's sake.

To my utter surprise, Maggie said calmly, "Sure. Actually, I'm the one who introduced them."

I felt my eyes widen. "You did?"

Was that the faintest hint of a smile at the corners of the other woman's wide mouth?

"Colin Novak is a doctor at the same hospital where my wife is a surgeon," she explained. "Jennifer and I have known him for years. He went through a bad divorce a couple of years ago, but was finally ready to get back out there. That's why I introduced him to Sela. He's a couple of years older than she is, grew up in Boston, loves to garden in his spare time. That's why I thought they'd get along well."

Apparently, they had...well enough that they'd decided to elope after only seeing each other for a month.

I had to ask. "Why didn't you tell the police about him?"

Maggie's gaze didn't waver. "Because Sela was trying to keep the whole thing quiet, and I wanted to respect her wishes."

"You're talking to me," I pointed out, and Maggie only shook her head.

"She trusted you enough to watch Lionel," she replied. "So that means I can trust you, too."

Fair enough. "Were you surprised about the two of them running off to Cancun to get married?" I asked next.

Maggie sent me a wry smile. "What do you think? I mean, Jennifer and I were happy for both of them, but we also thought they should take things a little more slowly than that, especially since Colin had told Jennifer more than once that there was no way he was getting married again without a pre-nup." Her shoulders lifted, and she added, "But I guess they were both so head over heels that he wasn't worried about any of that. And hey—they're both grown adults. They can make their own decisions, right?"

"Right," I murmured, even as my brain started

churning away, trying to figure out exactly what was going on here. I supposed it wasn't completely strange that Colin should have thrown caution to the wind—Sela was a very attractive woman and a business owner, so he probably wasn't worried about her taking him to the cleaners if their relationship did fall apart somewhere down the line.

But....

Something about the situation still didn't feel quite right. What if...?

What if Sela had cast a love spell on him? That sort of thing was generally frowned upon in the witch community, just because most of us didn't want to dabble in anything that involved such dubious consent, but that didn't mean it wouldn't still happen from time to time.

I really didn't want to think Sela was capable of such underhanded behavior, mostly because I thought Lionel was adorable and deserved a better mistress than that. But without her here to explain herself, I wasn't sure what else to think.

"It's a tragedy, though," Maggie commented. "About Anna, I mean. All those two had after their mother died was each other, and now with Anna gone...." The sentence trailed off, accompanied by a sorrowful shake of the head. "I suppose it's something of a blessing that at least Sela will have Colin to lean on once she finds out."

"He's a supportive guy?"

"Very," Maggie said, in emphatic tones that left little room for doubt. "He's a pediatric surgeon. Great with kids, great with people."

Well, it sounded as if Sela had made a perfect choice, even if she might have resorted to dubious means to bind Colin to her. And I still didn't know if that was the case at all. Theirs could have been one of those instant-attraction, once-in-a-lifetime kinds of things.

Sort of like what happened with me and Noah, I reminded myself, although it wasn't as if the two of us had eloped to Mexico or anything.

Would I have, if he'd asked?

I wanted to think I'd be far more sensible than Sela Warren...but I also needed to be honest with myself. There was definitely a greater-than-zero chance that if Noah came to me tonight and said he'd never met anyone like me and wanted to spend the rest of his life with me, I'd toss aside all those years of caution for a chance to be happy for the next five decades or so.

"But I really wish she would check in," Maggie continued. "It's just terrible that this happened to her sister, and she doesn't even know."

Because I'd been thinking the same thing for roughly the past twenty-four hours, I could only make a sound of assent. "What did Anna do?" I asked, curious.

"She had a little needlework shop down by the

harbor," Maggie replied. "Kind of a touristy thing, but the locals would also go there for embroidery supplies, that sort of stuff. It belonged to their mother. Technically, both girls inherited it after Enid passed away, but Sela wasn't interested in helping to run the business, and Anna bought her out. I think that's where Sela got some of the money to buy her house."

I'd been wondering about that. Sela's house on Abbott Street wasn't all that big, but it was updated and in a great location. Marblehead real estate prices were even crazier than prices in Salem, and a house there usually wasn't something a person could buy on their own.

"I guess the shop will be Sela's now, whether she wants it or not," Maggie added. "But first, she needs to get back here."

Which I supposed she would, even if she never checked all those voicemails, never realized what an awful tragedy was waiting for her once she returned to Marblehead. The twenty-sixth felt horribly far off, though. I needed to figure this out way before then, especially since there was no way to know if the witch who'd cast that death spell on Anna wasn't gearing up to take out the next person who got in her way.

"What about their father?" I asked, since I realized no one had ever mentioned him. In the witch world, that wasn't so strange, because we often had families without ever getting married—my bio-father was a sperm donor, and I knew next to nothing about him—but still, with their mother dead and Anna gone now as well, I had to wonder if the Warren sisters had any living relations. It was actually a little unusual that their mother had had two girls, because witches often stopped after their first child, not wanting to take the risk that a daughter of theirs might be born without any magic and would have to be raised away from the witch world, either fostered by relatives who were also mundies or put up for adoption.

"Sela never said anything about him," Maggie replied. "It sounded as if he didn't stick around very long after she was born."

Again, not that unusual. A witch might consider a man to be perfect genetic material to father her child, and still not want him to stay in her life after she had the daughter she wanted. It was much rarer for a witch to find someone she could trust enough to reveal everything about the magical world she inhabited, someone who would be at her side for her entire life. Valerie Monroe had been lucky enough to have a man like that, and so had Grace Bowersby, although both their husbands were now gone.

Anyway, it didn't sound as if the Warren sisters' father was anyone I needed to be concerned with, not if he'd been out of their lives for decades. No, there was something else going on here, something that had made Sela flee the country...something that had made Anna suffer such an untimely death.

"Any other relatives?" I asked, knowing I sounded a little desperate now, and again Maggie shook her head.

"Enid Warren was an only child," she replied. "And it sounded like her mother had been an only child, too. No cousins or anything that I ever heard of."

Which didn't surprise me too much. Still, that meant I really didn't have anyone else I could reach out to, no one who might be able to tell me something more about Sela, something that might provide the clues I needed.

"Did you know that the police couldn't find any information about Sela on any of the flight manifests for the planes that left Boston on the day she was supposed to be leaving for Cancun?"

Maggie appeared genuinely startled by that question. "No, I had no idea. That's strange."

"Do you think there's a chance she might have gone somewhere else and told everyone she was going to Cancun to throw people off the scent?"

Now Maggie's expression turned skeptical. "It sounds like you've been watching too many Jason Bourne movies."

I wished that were the case. Action-adventure

had never been my speed; I was more of a rom-com girl. "So, you don't think it's possible."

A long pause. Maggie shoved her hands into the pockets of her cargo pants, now looking worried. "I don't know," she said at last. "But if that's really what happened, I'd really like to know what scared her so much that she would take off like that."

So would I.

"Well, it was just a theory," I said, and tried my best to force a smile. "For all I know, she and Colin were planning to go to Cancun, but changed their minds at the last minute and had to go to New York to catch a plane or something. It happens."

This suggestion seemed to relax Maggie, because she also smiled a little as she said, "I could see that happening. I mean, if they were impulsive enough to run off and get married, then I could see them also making an abrupt decision like that, trying to be spontaneous."

I sincerely hoped that was what happened. After all, just because a situation looked sinister on the surface didn't necessarily mean something terrible had happened.

Voice turning brisk, Maggie said, "Well, I suppose we'll just have to wait to hear from Sela to get that particular mystery solved. But as far as your shop goes, it's a little dim in here, but I think we could still do something to green it up. Some snake plants for that dark corner, maybe a few pothos on those shelves—"

Since it seemed obvious she wanted to change the subject, I went along with her, nodding at her suggestions, telling her after we'd walked the shop that she could email me with her estimate. Once she was done, I thanked her for her time, then locked the front door and went to get the sleeping Lionel in his basket, calling for Milo as I did so.

I'd learned a few things...and had absolutely no idea what to do with them.

Chapter 8

Roman Holiday

ALTHOUGH NOAH AND I CHATTED BY TEXT after I got home, we both agreed we were tired that night and that we'd get together the next evening for some takeout at my place. It felt better to stay at home after being away from the house all day, just in case Lionel needed me close by after being at the shop for eight hours.

The next morning, he did seem a little perkier, although his minor improvement didn't relieve me very much, since he'd followed the same pattern the past couple of days. However, Milo convinced me to leave both of them at home.

"He just sleeps all the time anyway," the dog said, his big brown eyes beseeching. I could tell he didn't want to spend another day in the shop, and who could blame him? "And you can be home in ten minutes if anything goes wrong."

I wavered. While it wasn't any trouble to have Lionel in his basket at the store, I could tell Milo thought he had a responsibility to keep an eye on his fellow familiar. If Lionel came with me, then Milo would as well, even if he hated every minute of having to stay in his corner in the back of the shop.

"All right," I said, relenting. "But I'm coming home at lunch to check on you, and you need to call me the second anything goes wrong."

"It won't," Milo said stoutly. "If it does, though, I'll call you right away."

I supposed I had to be content with that promise. And it really did seem as if Lionel was doing better today, because he wanted to go out in the garden this morning and was actually able to climb the back steps under his own power, although he needed my help to get him back in the basket.

Driving in to work, though, I kept fretting whether I'd done the right thing. Yes, the house was only ten minutes from the shop, but a lot could happen in ten minutes.

Then again, if things went that sideways, I might not have been able to do anything in those ten minutes, anyway. It definitely took longer than that to get to Noah's clinic.

I also couldn't keep myself from brooding over my conversation with Maggie the afternoon before. It seemed more and more likely to me that Sela had broadcast the Cancun story because it was plausible, and that she and Colin had gone somewhere else entirely.

The only good thing about the whole mess was that Colin Novak definitely was a real person, and someone who sounded like a decent guy. He wasn't trying to take advantage of Sela so he could get his hands on her inheritance or anything like that. No, they'd fallen in love, and decided to make things permanent.

If only I could convince myself that their "insta-love" hadn't been magically motivated.

But for now, I needed to focus on the store. Sage wanted to know how Lionel was doing—I could tell she was surprised I hadn't brought him to work with me that day—and I told her he was improved enough that I thought it was okay for him to stay at home with Milo. Because she knew my adopted familiar was absolutely reliable and an excellent babysitter, she didn't seem to see anything wrong with my decision to leave them both at the house.

"It's good he's doing so much better," she said. "Although I kind of liked having him around."

As did I. At the same time, though, I knew I couldn't let myself get too attached. I always had to walk a fine line between caring for my familiars and getting so connected to them that I didn't want to let them go when the time came. Milo's case had been entirely different, because his mistress was dead and he had nowhere else to go.

But Sela was fine. Or at least, I hoped she was. Without hearing from her, it was impossible to know what might be happening in her life.

Where had she gone?

If I'd known her at all, I might have been able to hazard a guess. Maybe if I'd kept pressing Maggie, I would have been able to get her to tell me about any alternate places Sela might have wanted to visit. Nothing really kept witches from traveling, but we tended to be homebodies, not all that interested in globe-trotting. That Sela had left Massachusetts at all was a little astonishing, actually.

Or...*had* she left? Maybe she'd done her best to make everyone think she'd run off to Mexico, while instead she'd gone to ground somewhere nearby.

This seemed like a brilliant theory for all of two seconds...until I recalled how tense and jumpy she'd been. She hadn't been acting like someone who planned to stick close to home. No, she'd seemed like a woman who wanted to get far, far away, and fast.

Well, I could always try calling Maggie again and ask if she knew of any places that Sela talked about on a regular basis, destinations she'd dreamed of visiting but never had. For all I knew, the newlyweds were now wandering around

London or Paris, rather than basking in the sunshine of Mexico's eastern coast.

And actually, I got an email from Maggie a little after eleven that morning. Just a quote for a plant installation—much more reasonable than I'd thought it would be, which seemed like a sign that I should go ahead with the plan. It would be my way of saying thank-you for the information she'd provided.

I wrote back a reply saying the estimate sounded great, and that I was ready to go ahead whenever she had an opening in her schedule, then added a postscript.

Can you think of a place that Sela talked about wanting to visit? I was just thinking that could be where she and Colin went.

And then I sent the email, and prayed Maggie wouldn't keep me waiting for too long.

To my relief, she didn't. It was another twenty minutes before I could check my phone, since a large group came in—a family that had chosen Salem as the site of their reunion—and I was busy with them for a while.

But after they'd left and I was able to pull out my phone, I saw I had a response from Maggie.

Does next Thursday work for you? That's the soonest I have an opening in my schedule.

And I remember Sela talking about Rome and

the Isle of Capri several times. Do you think that's where she might have gone?

I didn't know and didn't have any real way of checking. Still, it was a lead...if a really tiny one.

Next Thursday works for me. We'll need to do it after five, though. And I don't know about Rome, but I think I know who to ask.

I sent the email, and then, before I could lose my nerve, I found the non-emergency number for the Salem police department online, and asked if I could speak to Derek Falco when the woman who answered the phone asked me how I wanted her to direct my call.

A pause, and then I heard his voice say, "Detective Falco here."

"Hi, Derek," I said, wishing I didn't feel so self-conscious about using his first name, even though he'd already asked me to do that very thing. "It's Charity."

"Oh...hi," he replied, sounding surprised. "How can I help you?"

Clearly, he'd guessed I wasn't calling to take him up on his offer of dinner. "It's about Sela Warren," I said. "I was just thinking about how Detective Finley said there wasn't any record of her flying out from Logan. Her business partner told me she'd always been interested in going to Rome. Do you think it's possible she went there and not to Cancun, and maybe flew from JFK or LaGuardia instead?"

For a few seconds, Derek didn't reply. When he spoke, his tone was still friendly, but now a little guarded as well. "Doing some investigating on your own?"

"Kind of," I said, since there didn't seem to be much point in denying what I'd been up to. "Mostly because she left her hedgehog with me, and I feel like I have a vested interest in finding out what's happening with her and why she isn't responding to any of her messages."

"I can understand that," he responded, and I relaxed a little. He didn't sound angry or annoyed about the way I'd started poking around, but maybe that was partly because this wasn't his investigation and he didn't need to worry about a civilian butting in. "Anyway, it's kind of a drive, but manageable. It still would have been easier to fly out of Logan, even if she might have had to change planes in New York or Philadelphia."

I wondered how Derek knew that, then thought that possibly he'd gone to Rome himself at some point. His last name was definitely Italian, so maybe he'd wanted to visit some long-lost relatives or something.

Not that it mattered. What mattered was that it was very possible that Colin and Sela had gotten in a car and driven the four-plus hours to New

York, and then boarded a plane to Rome...or Shanghai, or Sydney. With a couple of people who seemed so effectively disappeared, it was hard to say for sure.

"They would have had to rent a car, though," Derek added. "Chuck told me that both Sela Warren's and Colin Novak's vehicles were in their garages."

"Can you check on that?" I asked.

"Now that I know what to look for," he replied. "Let me ask around, and I'll get back to you."

"Thank you so much," I said. "I really appreciate this."

Another of those pauses. For a moment, I found myself wondering whether he was going to ask me out to dinner again as a way of saying thank-you for his help...and how in the world I would respond.

But then he said, "No problem. Give me an hour or so," and that seemed to be the end of it.

Well, at least until he got back to me with whatever information he found.

It was actually almost three hours before Derek came into the store. Sage had just gone out to get herself a mid-afternoon pick-me-up from the Star-bucks down on Washington Street, so luckily, we were alone in the shop.

Or maybe not so luckily, depending on how you looked at it.

He glanced at the counter, as if looking for Lionel's basket.

"Sela's hedgehog is at the house," I said. "Milo's keeping an eye on him."

If Derek thought there was anything strange about my recently adopted cocker spaniel watching over the hedgehog that had been left in my care, he didn't show it. Maybe a slight lift of his shoulders, and then he said, "Colin Novak and Sela Warren actually did rent a car from the Enterprise dealership down on Jefferson Avenue. They would have had to go there, since there isn't one in Marblehead. And the people at Enterprise will come pick you up if you request it, which explains why both Sela's and Colin's cars were still in their garages."

"Do you know where they went after that?"

He smiled. "Your hunch was right. They drove to JFK and turned the car in at the Enterprise kiosk there. Two hours later, they boarded a British Airways flight that went to Rome by way of London. It's going to be harder to figure out what happened from there, since I don't have access to either of their bank records to see which hotel they're staying in. But they're definitely not in Cancun."

"That's...amazing," I said, quite sincerely.

His smile broadened. "Just doing my job." He stopped there and shook his head a little. "All right, I guess it's not technically my job in this particular case, since I'm not on the team investigating Anna Warren's death. But this kind of information is easy enough to find with a little legwork."

Did that mean he'd gone in person to talk to the people at the local Enterprise outlet? Maybe.

I said, "I hope this isn't keeping you from any important cases of your own."

"Nope," he said cheerfully. "Things have been pretty quiet around here lately. I was glad to have the distraction."

Not sure what to do with that comment, I responded, "So...what happens now?"

"Well, this isn't a murder investigation," Derek said. "The M.E.'s report made that pretty obvious."

Obvious to a mundie, I thought. *Not so obvious to a witch.*

However, I knew I couldn't offer my own particular insights on that topic.

"So, while it's a little troubling that Sela Warren would go to such lengths to cover up her actual destination," he went on, "it's not as if anything illegal is going on here. I suppose it's possible that her sister didn't approve of her relationship with Colin Novak, and that's why Sela tried to hide where she was going. And I'll pass on this information to Detective Finley, for what it's worth."

Not that he would probably be able to do much with it. Sela wasn't a murder suspect, and the only reason the authorities wanted to get in touch with her was to let her know what had happened to her sister.

"Maybe he'll be able to get a hold of the authorities in Rome to see if they can help," I suggested.

I couldn't see Derek's face, but I got the impression he wasn't too hopeful about that. "Possibly," he allowed. "But Rome's a big city. And since no crime was committed, there's really not much urgency to finding Sela Warren. She's a grown woman and can do what she wants, even if her behavior might seem kind of odd to those of us looking in from the outside."

He had a point there. While there was a very good reason for trying to get in touch with Sela, in the end, she was an adult, hadn't broken any laws, and didn't have any reason to answer to any of the rest of us.

Well, except me, since I was taking care of Lionel. What would happen if she decided to stay in Italy indefinitely?

I told myself that wouldn't happen. Aside from any loyalty to her familiar, Sela owned a house and had a business in Marblehead. She would have to come back eventually, no matter how much she might be enjoying herself in Italy. And Colin was a pediatrician at the local hospital. I very much doubted he would abandon all that for a never-ending Roman holiday.

"Anyway," Derek said. "That's what I found. I'm not sure what to think about all of it, but—"

"It does seem a little strange," I remarked. "But people do what they do, I guess. Thanks again for digging all that up."

"Like I said, not a problem. Just let me know if you find anything else that you think might need some further investigation."

I told him I would, and he headed outside. Despite that promise, I doubted I would reach out to him again. After this, I had a feeling any further sleuthing on my part would only lead me deeper into witchy territory, a place Derek Falco absolutely could not go.

Sage came back in then, a go-cup from Star-bucks in her hand. She tended to alternate between plain old iced tea and some kind of sweet coffee for her afternoon caffeine fix, but because today's beverage had a basic flat top and not one of those dome-shaped things designed to protect the whipped cream inside, I guessed she'd opted for iced tea.

"Detective Falco was here?"

She must have spotted him walking back to his

car, so there wasn't any way I could try to cover up his visit. "Yes," I said, doing my best to sound casual. "He came by to tell me a few things he'd found out about Sela Warren."

This explanation must have sounded reasonable enough to my assistant, because she didn't make any further comments about his "hotness," and only tilted her head in a thoughtful way. "Like what?"

I'd already planned to pass the information along to the other members of the coven, so there wasn't much point in trying to hide anything. "That Sela is in Rome, not Cancun, and she flew out of JFK."

Sage's fawn-brown eyebrows lifted. "Why would she do something like that?"

"I'm not sure," I replied. "Best guess is that she was trying to make it harder for anyone tracking her movements to figure out where she was going."

That comment earned me an amused little snort. "What, is she trying to hide from the FBI or something?"

"I doubt it," I said. "I mean, Detective Falco could figure out where she'd gone, so this isn't a CIA-level cover-up or anything. But something weird is definitely going on."

"There's been a lot of that lately," Sage remarked, then took a pull of her iced tea through its straw. "And here I thought Salem had to be one of the most boring places in the world to live."

Since I'd harbored that same notion most of my time in high school—even though Sage was in her early twenties—I didn't bother to disabuse her of it. No, there wasn't what you could call a lively club scene, and if you wanted to see any big-name acts, you had to travel to Boston, but there was still plenty to do in Salem, especially if you were a history buff. You practically couldn't turn around without hitting a historic marker or a museum.

"Well, technically, Sela's from Marblehead, but yeah," I said. "I could do with a little more peace and quiet myself. Still, unless she decides to get in touch after all—which I'm doubting more and more every day—there's not much any of us can do except wait it out."

"And hope Lionel's okay," Sage responded.

"So far, so good," I said. At least, there hadn't been any calls from Milo, which seemed to indicate the little hedgehog was holding his own for now.

How long that would last was anyone's guess.

But the rest of the afternoon was quiet enough, although something made me want to linger at the shop after Sage left, even though I should have been itching to get home and check on Lionel.

Noah and I had tentative plans to have him come over to my house for takeout, but he wouldn't be there until six-thirty until the earliest, which meant I had a little time.

Time for what, I wasn't sure. Something in me, some kind of gut instinct, was telling me I needed to be here at the store, although I had absolutely no idea why. Contrary to popular belief, most witches weren't psychic, and I knew I sure as hell wasn't.

But....

Something was making me linger at the shop, something way beyond the need to straighten up the hanging packets of herbs on one rack, a display that had gotten turned into a mess after a bunch of high school kids decided it would be funny to rearrange the little packets to have the initials of the herbs spell out rude comments, rather than having them in the proper alphabetical order.

Was I that big a jerk in high school?

I didn't think so. Mostly, I was the quiet girl who tried to sit in the back of the class and not get called on. I was a decent enough student, but I'd been so worried about my classmates discovering I was actually a witch that I'd always done my best to blend into the background.

Just as I was finishing up with that task, I heard a tentative knock at the front door. I headed over, ready to tell the person there that it was way past business hours and that they'd have to come back in the morning.

The words died on my lips, though, when I realized the woman who'd knocked at the door was Elise Figg.

Startled, I unlocked the door and let her in. "Hi, Elise," I said. "What's up?"

Usually, Elise was a fairly self-assured person. About ten years younger than my mother, she had brown hair and gray eyes, and always looked as though she knew exactly what she was doing.

Now, though, she cast a nervous glance around the store, as if wanting to reassure herself that we were alone there even despite the shop being closed nearly twenty minutes earlier.

"I need to talk to you," she said, and I tilted my head, knowing I probably looked just as puzzled as I felt.

"About...?"

Once again, she looked around. "About Sela's familiar," she replied.

"What about him?" I asked. "Do you know a way to lift the hex?"

Her gray eyes met mine, worried and yet pleading at the same time. "I can lift it," she said. "Because I'm the one who cast it."

Chapter 9

Crime and Punishment

FOR THE LONGEST MOMENT, I COULD ONLY stare at Elise in shock. "*You* put the hex on Lionel?" I demanded. "But...why?"

"It's nothing I would have done if I wasn't forced into it," she said, tone earnest, dark eyes fixed on mine. "But about a little over a week ago, several days before Sela dropped Lionel off with you, I found a note in my mailbox. The person who wrote it said they knew I was the one who'd cast the spell that killed Brian Alatorre, and that they'd go to the police in Chicago and tell them all about it if I didn't do as I was told."

Although the inside of the shop was warm enough—verging on uncomfortable, actually, because the timer on the thermostat raised the temperature to eighty at a quarter after the hour to save energy when the store was closed—a shiver worked its way down my spine.

Who could possibly have known that Elise Figg was the person who'd made sure Brian Alatorre could never talk about his powers...or the witch world in general?

"I assume the note wasn't signed," I commented.

"No," she said. "It wasn't handwritten—it was printed on plain white paper, probably from a laser printer. Anyway, I told myself to ignore it, that there was no way to connect me to Brian Alatorre's death, not when magic was involved and I'd never gone near the man."

She sounded so casual when talking about killing a man in cold blood. But then, in Elise's eyes —and the eyes of the rest of the coven, if I wanted to be truthful about it—Brian hadn't been a man at all, but the equivalent of a rabid animal that needed to be put down.

"But then I got another note the next day," she went on. "That one spelled out exactly how they would incriminate me in Brian's death, how they said they would tell the police to look for my finger-prints on the life support equipment that had been in his room."

"Is that possible?" I asked. Not that I knew much about hospital procedures, but I had to believe any equipment that had been used on him would have been sanitized and prepped for the next patient who needed it.

Elise's thin shoulders lifted. "I don't know for sure," she replied. "The note made it sound as if everything had been put in storage after his death. Anyway, the second note said that if I wanted to make all this go away, then I needed to put a hex on Lionel, one that would cause misfortune to occur to anyone close to him. And if I didn't comply within twenty-four hours, then the person who wrote the note would go to the police."

I didn't bother to ask whether Elise had caved to these demands. The mere fact that Lionel was currently suffering under a hex was evidence enough.

"So...why come to me now?" I said. "Aren't you worried that if you lift the hex, the person blackmailing you will go to the police, anyway?"

That question got me a crooked little smile. "Maybe," she responded. "But technically, I did what they said. I cast the hex. The note I got didn't say anything about lifting it."

True. A sudden thought occurred to me, and I said, "So...you're the one who prevented the coven from lifting the hex the other night?"

"Yes," she said, looking guilty. "I was worried about what might happen to me if I was the one who broke the curse, so instead of lending my own strength to the spell, I was feeding it directly into the hex, strengthening it." Even more shamefaced, she went on, "Then I heard about how Lionel wasn't doing well, and I knew it had to have something to do with the way I'd strengthened the hex. It was never supposed to rebound on him, but I think that's exactly what happened. That's why I came here today. I'd feel terrible if something awful happened to Lionel when he's absolutely innocent."

I reflected that people could be wonderfully inconsistent sometimes. As far as I could tell, Elise didn't bear any particular guilt over what she'd done to Brian Alatorre, but she couldn't bear the thought of hurting a hedgehog.

However, I certainly wasn't going to argue. Elise Figg had done this...and now it looked as though she was willing to undo it.

"All right," I said. "Let me lock up, and then we'll head over to my house."

Both the familiars looked surprised to see me appear with Elise in tow, because I honestly didn't have that many visitors.

Except Noah, of course, but he was a special case.

"Elise is here to help you with your hex, Lionel," I told him. Driving over, I'd decided it was better not to say that she'd been responsible for the curse in the first place. No, all he needed to know was that she was going to make him well again. After that was done, then I'd have to decide whether to out Elise to the rest of the coven, or whether it would be better to let it go now that she'd done the right thing.

First, though, I had to make sure she actually could lift the hex.

The hedgehog looked up at Elise with his bright black eyes. He really did seem a bit better today, although I got the impression he still had spent most of his time in his basket. "Is she a witch doctor?" he asked me.

Despite the seriousness of the situation, my mouth twitched a little. "Something like that," I said gravely. "Is it okay if she puts her hand on your head?"

"If that'll make me feel better."

"It will," I promised, then nodded at Elise, signaling it was all right for her to proceed.

She squatted down next to the hedgehog—she was wearing a black sleeveless dress, and so the position looked a little more graceful than it might have if she'd been in jeans, like I was—and laid her hand on top of Lionel's spiky head. Her eyes closed and her lips moved, but I couldn't hear what she was saying.

Most likely on purpose; I doubted she wanted Lionel...or Milo...to realize that she wasn't casting a healing spell, but instead was uttering the words that would reverse the hex she'd placed on the hedgehog a week ago.

As soon as she was done speaking, Lionel gave a shake, as though trying to cast off something that had been weighing on him. His eyes seemed to brighten, and he climbed out of his basket and rolled around on the floor for a few seconds before springing back to his feet.

"I feel much better now!" he exclaimed.

"Good," Elise said as she rose to her feet. "Then the spell worked. The hex is lifted, and you won't have to worry about it anymore."

Lionel danced over to Milo, who'd been looking on with a bright doggy smile on his lips. "Let's go outside, Milo!"

The dog gave me a very brief glance, and I nodded, letting him know it was okay to take his fellow familiar out in the backyard. They hurried toward the kitchen and the door that opened to the garden, and were gone.

I looked back at Elise. "You're sure he's going to be okay?"

"He'll be fine," she said. "Now I just have to

hope that whoever coerced me into casting that hex won't find out it's been lifted."

I hoped so, too. While I couldn't condone what Elise had done, I also didn't want the black-mailer to come after her.

Especially not when I had questions of my own.

"Is that the only thing the blackmailer asked you to do?" I said, and she gave me a level stare, clearly understanding what I'd just asked.

"I had nothing to do with Anna Warren's death," Elise replied, her tone flat, emphatic. "I was told to put a hex on Lionel, so I did. That seemed to be the end of it. I couldn't really understand why anyone would want to do that to him, and I still don't."

Neither did I. There seemed to be a lot of missing pieces to this particular puzzle, and I wasn't sure whether I'd ever be able to put them in their proper places.

"You know I'll have to say something to the coven about this," I told her, and she shook her head.

"Don't bother—I'll tell them myself."

I sent her a very direct look. "You're sure?"

Her mouth lifted in a bitter curve. "Oh, I'm sure. Because if I don't, you will, and that'll make things even worse."

Before I could respond, Elise turned away from

me and headed out the front door. She'd insisted on driving her own car, so it wasn't as though she needed to wait on anyone for a ride.

Would she ask the coven to assemble so she could confess to everyone in person, or would she contact each member separately in order to give them an individual apology? I didn't much care how she did it, as long as we all knew the truth eventually.

What would happen in the end, I didn't know for sure. There were rare accounts of covens expelling members for gross misconduct, but I had no idea whether this business with the hex would be enough for everyone else to eject her. In general, covens were democratic entities, with all the members having equal votes when it came to important matters like this, so we'd all have to come to some kind of agreement as to an appropriate punishment.

But I'd let wiser minds than mine figure that out. For me, the important thing was that Elise had come clean...and that Lionel appeared to be completely cured.

I went into the kitchen and looked out the window. There were Milo and Lionel, playing some kind of tag on a sunny patch of grass. They both looked utterly and completely happy, and I let out a relieved little breath.

It appeared I didn't need to worry about Lionel

anymore...but now I had the additional mystery of Elise's blackmailer to add to the ongoing conundrum of who'd killed Anna Warren, and why.

Well, I could put that aside for one evening.

I hoped.

Noah was very relieved to see Lionel full of energy, happily munching away at his dinner. "You said you came home, and he was like this?"

I nodded. There was no way to tell him that the hex which had been placed on the hedgehog had now been lifted, so it seemed safest to make it seem as if Lionel had experienced some kind of spontaneous remission.

"Yes, he's acting like his old self. Do you have any idea what could have made him behave like that in the first place?"

Poor Noah looked positively flummoxed. He continued to stare down at the hedgehog for a second or two, then said, "No, I don't. Then again, I don't have a lot of experience with hedgehogs. He could have eaten something that made him listless and tired, and then once it was all the way out of his system, he was able to get back to his old self."

"That makes sense," I said. "After all, I don't know what he got into before Sela dropped him off."

A nod, and then we went on to discuss whether we wanted pizza or Thai. We both decided on pizza—mostly because the pizza place delivered directly rather than requiring us to use DoorDash, thus simplifying the process—and that seemed to be that.

All the same, I couldn't completely let my guard down. Even if Lionel was cured, there was still a killer out there somewhere...and a blackmailer.

But I told myself it would probably take the blackmailer a while to even figure out that the hex was gone. I hadn't brought Lionel to the store today, so having him stay at the house from now on wouldn't seem too strange. Unless they were paying very close attention, they might not notice anything in his status had changed at all.

Fingers crossed.

The next day was the summer solstice, an important holiday for any practicing witch. To tell the truth, I'd been so preoccupied with Lionel's health and Anna's death—and Sela's disappearance—that I'd almost forgotten the solstice was upon us.

However, I got a text from Valerie Monroe

right after lunch, reminding me we were meeting at her house that evening.

Seven o'clock at my place. Wear your good clothes. Everyone needs to be there...we have business to attend to.

I assumed that ominous allusion to "business" meant that we'd be dealing with Elise Figg in some way. What shape those repercussions would take, I didn't know for sure. She might simply be shunned for a time, not allowed to have dealings with anyone else in the coven or to take part in our rituals until we all decided it was all right to allow her to take part again.

Or the elder witches—my mother and Valerie and Grace—could determine it was better to just kick Elise out altogether, forcing her to go solo, or, more likely, to find a different coven that would take her in. I couldn't say the three of them would be out of bounds for doing so, but....

Elise had seemed genuinely remorseful for what she'd done, but it was possible no other covens would take her in after they learned what she'd done. We had four operating in the general Salem area, and we were all on friendly terms. When it came to who was in or out of a particular coven, it was more a matter of style rather than a difference of bedrock principles.

I kind of doubted anyone in Salem would have

approved of Elise caving to a blackmailer and casting a hex on a completely innocent hedgehog.

But since I wouldn't know the outcome of the situation unless I attended the ritual, I went home and changed out of my jeans and sandals and summery top—black, true, but sleeveless and light-weight—and into the long black dress and lace-up boots I usually wore to coven meetings. My pointy hat would get to ride on the front seat, since trying to wear it while I was driving was a total pain.

I'd already told Noah I was having dinner with my mother that night, and he'd told me to have a good time, and maybe we'd get together on Thursday. Just something else that was completely refreshing about the guy—he always seemed happy when we were able to see each other, but he also never pressed me when I had my own plans, didn't act needy or upset that I'd had a life of my own before we got together.

Could someone actually be so perfect?

It sure appeared that way.

Milo and Lionel seemed fine with me going out for the evening—probably because I ate an early dinner and fed the dog some table scraps, and let both of them out again to enjoy the mild tempera-tures before I had to head over to Valerie's house. She had a gorgeous old Victorian right next door to the tea shop she'd once owned and had passed on to Stella...although I'd heard Valerie was back working at the store, since Stella was going to be home with baby Aurora for at least the next six months, if not more.

Because of making sure the two familiars had a little time outside before I left, I was the last one to arrive, and had to park halfway down the block. Witch hat in one hand and purse dangling from the other, I made my way to the front porch of Valerie's house, trying not to feel self-conscious. Salem was full of women who went around in tall, pointy hats—some of them actual witches, some of them mundies who enjoyed playacting—so it wasn't as though any of Valerie's neighbors would have paid any attention to me. Still, while I was a witch born and bred, I didn't like to advertise it.

Call me a stealth witch.

I'd been coming here long enough that I knew I didn't need to ring the doorbell; Valerie would have left the door unlocked for me. Likewise, pausing in the foyer so I could put on my hat and adjust it while I stood in front of the large pier mirror also felt like second nature to me. Once I was ready to join the meeting, I headed to the door that opened on the cellar stairs, and made my way down the steep steps.

As I'd guessed, everyone was already there... well, everyone except Stella, who was home with her baby, and Sage, who often missed our meetings...although Elise stood off to one side, wearing a shamefaced expression that was very different from her usual slightly mischievous mien. No one seemed inclined to talk to her, although Valerie beamed at me as I appeared and said, "Ah, Charity. Good. Now we can get started."

Like Grace's basement, Valerie's had been painted in a jewel tone as well, this one rich amethyst instead of deep emerald. Candles flickered on the walls, and the space smelled spicy and autumnal, a mixture of cinnamon and cloves and what I thought might be nutmeg. It all felt awfully cozy for what was probably going to turn into a disciplinary meeting, but I figured that was just how Valerie rolled.

As if by instinct, everyone moved to form a circle, with the now even warier-looking Elise standing in the middle.

"Elise, tell us your crimes," Grace Bowersby said.

The other witch lifted her chin. "How long have you got?"

Next to me, my mother might have chuckled a bit, not loud enough for Grace—who stood across the circle—to have heard.

My mother never had been the type to stand on ceremony...even in a situation as grave as this.

"The current one will suffice," Tonya Willis said crisply.

"I cast a hex on an innocent creature," Elise

announced. She still held her chin high, telling me that, while she knew she was in the wrong here, she also wasn't going to act like some sort of cowed prisoner. "It was wrong. My only defense is that I was coerced into it, or risk having the Chicago police department open an investigation into me." A pause, and she sent a sharp glance around the circle. "I think we all know why that wouldn't be a very good idea."

"We do," Tonya said, although she didn't sound particularly moved by Elise's argument. "And while we understand the need to keep the authorities from investigating any of us too closely, you still showed a profound error in judgment by not bringing your predicament to the attention of the rest of the coven. We could have helped you."

"How?"

Grace Burrows and Valerie Monroe exchanged a weighty glance, while Izzy Halloran stayed quiet, clearly wishing to be a spectator and nothing more. "We could have cast a spell on the blackmail note you received," Grace said, "and attempted to find out who actually sent it."

"You think I didn't try that?" Elise retorted, her expression now annoyed. "I couldn't pick up anything from the letter."

"So, it was sent by another witch?" Tonya inquired. Now she was frowning, obviously troubled.

Elise's thin shoulders lifted in a small shrug. "I don't know. Maybe. Or maybe my magic just failed me there."

"All the more reason why you should have come to us," Grace said.

"Well, she didn't," I put in. "So instead of arguing about what might have been, maybe we should focus on what we're going to do next."

Tonya lifted an eyebrow. Something in her expression seemed to indicate she wasn't too happy with me for that particular observation, and yet I only stared back at her, trying to look calm and cool. Maybe I was the youngest person here, but as a full member of the coven, I was equally entitled to offer my own opinions.

My mother smiled. "Charity is right. What's done is done. Now it's our job to decide what sort of punishment Elise should face."

I didn't like the sound of that, even though I knew the coven was within its rights to punish Elise for her actions. "Why worry about any punishment at all?" I asked. "She came clean about what she did, and she removed the hex on Lionel. He seems to be just fine, so I'm not sure it's a good idea to get all draconian about this."

"I'm surprised you would say that," Tonya responded. "Considering that Sela's hedgehog was in your care, and you personally suffered the ill effects of the curse. It was sheer luck that kept you from being seriously hurt."

Well, all right, that was true. But since I'd managed to escape more or less unscathed, I supposed I didn't see the point in still trying to bring down the hammer on Elise's head.

"I guess I don't carry grudges," I said. "So in this particular case, I'd say it was no harm, no foul. It wasn't as if she tried to keep hiding what she'd done. No, she told the truth and said she was prepared to face the consequences...whatever those might be."

Valerie leaned over and murmured something to Grace, who gave a reluctant nod.

"This isn't the kind of thing we can just let go," she said. "But you're right—there are extenuating circumstances. One could argue that Elise was trying to protect all of us, since we don't know what might have happened if a detective from the Chicago police department really had started poking around and asking questions. So, I think we can find a middle ground here."

"Elise Figg," Valerie said, her voice deeper and sterner than it had been a moment earlier. Elise stood up a little straighter, head still up, as though she knew the time had come when she would have to meet her fate. "You are shunned for a period of one month. You may not participate in any cere-monies, and you may not use any magic save for what is required to keep yourself and this coven safe. Do you understand?"

A single nod. I could tell from the tension in her slender throat how much Elise hated to stand there and accept her punishment...but I could also see from the way she remained silent that she wasn't about to argue with the coven's decision.

"Then you can go," Grace said, her voice now almost too kind, as if she was doing her best to soften the blow that had just been delivered. "We need to begin the solstice ceremony now, but we can't have you here to participate."

Another nod. In a murmur, Elise said, "Thank you," and then hurried up the stairs.

"Well, that's done," my mother remarked, her brisk tone a marked contrast to the near-whisper Elise had used a moment earlier. "Now it's time to get down to business."

We all joined hands, and Tonya said, "Let us honor the turning of the year, the shift back to the darker months. Let us combine our magic as we celebrate the power of the sun while it still showers us with its bounty."

I held hands with my mother and with Grace Bowersby, and did my best to focus on the words of the ceremony as Tonya continued to lead the coven in its solstice observance. The whole time, though, I couldn't quite keep my brain from picking away at the problem of that ransom note.

Had a witch really sent it? But why? Why would one of our own take the risk of attracting police scrutiny to our small community?

Just like all the other questions that had been plaguing me lately, I doubted I'd find an answer to this one anytime soon.

Chapter 10

Going to Ground

The next day, everything seemed relatively normal. Yes, it felt strange to think that Elise Figg wouldn't have any interactions with the rest of the coven for the next thirty days, but really, it wasn't as though we were in each other's laps all the time. We all had our own lives to live, our own problems, our own minor triumphs.

Not that I had much of anything to feel triumphant about at the moment. Yes, I was thrilled that Lionel was better—and that he was still happy and perky when he woke up this morning, telling me the hex really was gone—but I hadn't heard anything from Sela. I guessed she planned to stay incommunicado the entire time she was in Rome, lest anyone try to interrupt her honeymoon.

Did she feel guilty about pulling the wool over

all our eyes? Or was she just relieved that no one knew where she really was?

Hard to say, because I didn't know her well enough to even hazard a guess. And although Derek Falco knew the truth about Sela's current location, I didn't know if he would pass that information along to Detective Finley. Anna's death, for Chuck Finley, was only a sad footnote to a quiet life, since he had no reason to believe foul play had been involved, not when all the physical evidence pointed to a catastrophic aneurysm.

I knew better, of course, but I couldn't tell him that it was imperative to get hold of Sela somehow, that she might also be at risk, because doing so would mean telling him that Anna Warren's aneurysm had been caused by dark magic. Most likely, he'd think I was nuts, and yet there was no way I could take even the infinitesimally small chance that he might believe me.

And as much as I tried to mull over everything Maggie Phillips had told me regarding the Warren sisters, I couldn't find a single thing about either one of them that should have been cause for murder...unless, of course, some other witch had coveted Colin Novak for herself, and had been furious when he ran off with Sela. Even if that proved to be the case, it didn't explain why Anna had been targeted and not Sela.

Unless the rival witch was angry enough that

she'd decided the entire Warren family needed to be wiped off the face of the earth. If that proved to be the case, then I supposed I could see why Sela had done everything she could to conceal where she was really going.

It was pretty hard to hit someone with a curse if you didn't know where they were. Not impossible, but not the sort of thing most witches would try, because not having an obvious target meant you might hit the wrong person entirely, or worse, have it rebound on you.

Sage had heard about the incident with Elise from her mother, although she hadn't attended our gathering the night before. Her absence hadn't surprised me too much—my assistant was a member of the coven, but she often skipped our meetings and only dropped in when she felt like it. In stricter covens, that sort of behavior might have led to a shunning of her own.

We were a pretty casual group, though, and acknowledged that people had their own lives and could come and go as they pleased. Usually, Sage would be present for something as important as a solstice observance, but she'd gone with a group of friends to a concert in Boston and had come back late. Unlike me, who'd always been wary of getting too close to mundies and letting something important slip, she didn't seem to have a problem with hanging out with mostly regular folks. That could have been because there simply weren't any other witches in town around her age—Stella Monroe and I had been lucky that we were born within six months of each other—but I guessed Sage would have had a lot of mundane friends even if she'd had enough other Salem witches her own age to create a coven of her own.

She was a few minutes late to work, which didn't surprise me, considering she probably hadn't gotten home until close to one o'clock last night. Despite that, she looked chipper enough, although her expression grew sober as she spoke.

"I heard about Elise," she said. "I can't believe she would do that to Lionel."

"I didn't want to believe it, either," I replied. No one had come into the shop yet, which was why we were both able to speak freely. "But it's the truth. I watched her lift the hex. And now he's doing great, so that's something."

"At least she did the right thing in the end," Sage commented. "That's why I'm kind of surprised the coven agreed to shun her for a month. It seems kind of extreme to me."

Since I'd thought pretty much the same thing, I made a sound of agreement. "I know. And I tried to speak up for her. But the old guard wanted to make sure she knew she screwed up pretty badly."

Which she had. I couldn't argue with that. What I had a problem with was meting out such a harsh punishment to someone who'd done her best to correct her wrongdoing.

"What happens if I bump into Elise at the grocery store or something?" Sage asked next. "Am I supposed to just ignore her? I've never had to deal with anything like this before."

Neither had I, because the coven had never had any reason to shun someone during the entire time I'd been a member.

"I suppose you can just say hi," I responded. "I mean, it would look even more obvious if you tried to pretend she didn't exist, since everyone knows she's been a friend of your family for years. Just don't try to prolong the contact or anything like that."

Sage pursed her lips, head tilted slightly, which told me she wasn't sure she particularly liked that piece of advice. However, she didn't argue, and I guessed she knew deep down that I was right, that we all needed to act normal while at the same time making it clear to Elise that she was still reaping what she'd sown.

A couple of customers—a man and woman in their early forties, probably tourists since I'd never seen them before—came into the shop, and Sage and I had to halt our conversation there. Just as well, since I knew I was in the unenviable position of having to defend the coven's decision, even while I disagreed with it.

Noah texted me a little before twelve, asking if I wanted to come over, and I replied immediately.

Would love to. Takeout?

No, I'll barbecue. My last app't is at 4:15, so I have some extra time this afternoon.

A barbecue at Noah's place sounded like the perfect antidote to all the angst I'd experienced over the past few days. At the same time, I wondered whether I should say anything to him about the way Derek Falco had come by the store the day before.

Why not? I argued with myself. *He wasn't asking you out on another date. He just wanted to discuss Sela's case with you.*

Put that way, the whole thing seemed pretty innocent...which it was. No reason for me to tie myself into knots about it. Besides, talking over the situation with Noah might lead me to some new insights. Getting someone else's opinion always helped.

Six-thirty?

See you then.

With that settled, I found myself relaxing a bit. I knew Milo and Lionel would be fine, even though I guessed my adopted familiar would probably rather be over at Noah's house, begging for bits of burger—or whatever it was he decided to barbecue tonight—rather than staying home. However, while Noah loved all animals, I thought bringing the hedgehog along might be asking a bit much. Although I'd assured Noah that Lionel was just fine now, he would still probably be extra vigilant, wanting to keep an eye on the tiny animal to make sure he really was okay.

And though we were busy enough that day that I couldn't spare too many extra thoughts on the mystery of Anna Warren's death, something about the whole situation still kept bothering me.

Was the person who'd blackmailed Elise and who'd killed Anna the same witch?

It felt like it to me, even though, if asked, I probably couldn't have come up with any concrete facts to support that itch from my intuition.

We had a lull in the middle of the afternoon, one where I asked Sage to keep an eye on things out front so I could go downstairs to the stockroom. The secondary stockroom, that is, the one that I only visited a few times a month. Most of the time, any shipments went into the storage area at the back of the shop, but when I got a particularly big delivery, I put it down in the cellar where it wouldn't take up any necessary space. And because the huge order of mason jars and bottles I'd placed several months ago had decided to finally make an appearance today, that meant I had to unpack them and put them on the shelving units I kept down there, waiting for the time when they'd be filled with one of my various elixirs and then put on sale.

The basement always felt cold and damp, no big surprise, considering it was some fifteen feet underground. I had a dehumidifier running there year-'round, but somehow, it never seemed to completely remove the slightly mildewy scent that hung on the air no matter how often I wiped the shelves and the walls down with a mild bleach solution.

Today, the UPS driver had shown up with the unwieldy boxes right at lunch. He knew me and knew his route, so he'd taken everything downstairs for me while I dealt with customers. Now, though, it was quiet enough that I thought I could do a quick unboxing rather than have to stay late. Definitely didn't want to do that today, not when I had a date with Noah.

At least there was plenty of room on my storage racks; I'd waited longer than I should to place this order and had already run through a good three-quarters of my previous stash. I worked as quickly and carefully as I could, since, even though I knew Sage could handle anything upstairs short of two tour busloads of people showing up at the same time, I kind of hated it down in the basement. The place always gave me the creeps, no matter how many times I told myself that it wasn't haunted and I had nothing concrete to worry about.

Well, until a large rat decided to run right across my sandal-clad foot.

I let out a scream and jumped backward—not the most brilliant idea, because I stumbled right into one of my shelving units, sending it teetering on two of its feet before it tumbled over, smacking right into the wall immediately behind it. Luckily, I'd barely started to load the shelves, so only five or six bottles got smashed, but—

Wait a second.

The walls of the basement were uneven plaster that had been hastily smeared over old bricks and stone. When I righted the shelving unit and awkwardly set it out of the way, I could see that the plaster had crumbled—as had the patchwork wall beneath, revealing a yawning, dark passageway of some kind.

Sage's voice drifted down the basement stairs, worried. "Charity? Is everything okay?"

"It's fine," I called back up to her. "I just had a close encounter with a rat, but I'm all right. Can you hold down the fort up there for a while longer while I get things cleaned up?"

"Sure," she responded at once. "It's pretty quiet right now...well, except for the screaming."

"Very funny."

I heard her chuckle, but after that, things went

quiet again.

As soon as I knew she wasn't listening, I turned back toward the hole in the wall. It was irregular in shape, just a little bit taller than I was.

What the hell?

Clearly, someone had wanted to hide what was back there. How long it had been covered up, I wasn't sure, but I'd owned the store for about five years, and the previous owner, a man named Emerson Gates, who'd occupied the space since the late 1980s, had never said anything about a passageway in the basement. He'd been a dealer in antique musical instruments, and I doubted he would have ever stored anything valuable down here, considering how damp it was and what those kinds of conditions could do to a delicate item like a harp or a violin.

But Salem was an old, old place, and had more than its share of secrets.

Because of a particularly harrowing incident a couple of years ago when the power had failed and I'd been stuck down here in the dark, I always kept a hand-cranked flashlight near the stairs in case of emergency. I got it now, cranked it for a minute to get it up to full power, and then went over to the opening in the wall and shone the light inside.

The beam revealed a narrow passageway not much more than three feet across and a little more than five and a half feet high. As far as I could tell, it extended about three yards or so before jogging to the left and disappearing into darkness. The walls in there were also a hodgepodge of stone patched here and there with uneven brick, just like the crumbled wall in my basement.

Did I want to find out where the passage went?

Remembering the rat who'd run across my sandal-clad foot a few minutes earlier, not really. At the same time, though, I knew I couldn't just let this go, not when I had so many unanswered questions hanging over my head. This might not have anything at all to do with Anna's death and Sela's flight to Rome, but all the same, I still thought I should come back and go exploring with the much bigger flashlight I kept at the house...and with my feet safely covered in at least sneakers, if not hiking boots.

But I had a date with Noah tonight.

Well, bring him along, I thought. *He'd be more than a match for any rats down there.*

As soon as the thought passed through my head, however, I realized I'd have to shoot it down. There wasn't much reason for me to believe there was anything especially witchy about the passageway—the stories about the tunnels under Salem were common knowledge, and I knew they had been built to smuggle opium and spices back in the day, and were reputed to have been part of the Underground Railroad at some point as well.

Still, I couldn't risk having Noah run into something that looked at all suspicious, especially when
all my instincts kept trying to tell me this needed to
be investigated.

No, I'd have to come back tonight after our
date. At least we both had to be at work the next
day, so this wouldn't be one of those times where I
stayed at his house well past midnight.

Although I doubted Sage would have any
reason to come down here, I pushed the metal rack
back into place as best I could, then got out the
broom and dustpan I kept in a corner and swept
up the broken glass. I'd have to leave it in the
dustpan until I could bring a trash can down here
—I'd been meaning to leave a bin in the basement
permanently and kept forgetting—but at least I'd
made something of an effort to get things tidied up.

I climbed the stairs, emerged at the back of the
store, then headed up front toward the cash register. Sage was helping a customer, but as soon as
she'd bagged the woman's purchases and handed
over her receipt, she turned back toward me,
expression expectant.

"A rat?"

I nodded. "A big one."

She shuddered. "No wonder I never go down
there."

That worked just fine for me. Grinning, I said,
"I wouldn't advise it."

We had a fairly steady stream of patrons after that, and soon enough, it was five o'clock and time to lock up. I said goodbye to Sage and headed home, my brain going about a million miles an hour. Who had connected that passageway to the shop? As far as I knew, my little block of buildings had never been part of the smuggler's tunnels that ran under Salem. Then again, it wasn't as if the smugglers had published a diagram of their labyrinth in the local newspaper. That would have defeated the purpose.

I went home to find Milo and Lionel asleep in front of my dead television. Clearly, they hadn't been watching *Animal Planet,* but it seemed as if they'd congregated there anyway out of habit.

"Want to go outside?" I asked, and they both opened their eyes. Yes, Milo at least could come and go through the doggy door as he pleased, but he'd always enjoyed the ritual of being let out into the backyard.

"Yes!" Lionel replied at once, and got to his tiny little feet. His black eyes shone up at me, and I could tell that his nap had been that and nothing more, because he certainly looked full of energy now, thanks to Elise removing that awful hex.

Milo also got up, although a little more slowly. "How was work?"

"Just fine," I said. I wondered briefly whether I should bring him along on my foray into the tunnels tonight, then decided against it. Milo would probably be valuable on that kind of expedition, but I didn't want to leave Lionel at home alone. Maybe I was worrying about nothing, but with a blackmailing witch still roaming around out there somewhere, I didn't think it was a good idea for him to be completely unprotected.

For a moment, my adopted familiar looked at me carefully, head cocked, as though he was trying to decide whether I was keeping something from him. But then he gave the doggy equivalent of a shrug and followed Lionel into the kitchen.

I went ahead and opened the back door for them, and went to the refrigerator and poured myself some water while the two familiars wandered around on the grass, Milo sniffing away, Lionel just looking happy to be outside in the fresh air. The sight made me smile, despite everything I had pressing on my mind.

Should I tell someone else about the passageway I'd found? My mother would warn me to stay away, but maybe Grace Bowersby would have some useful information to impart on the subject. She did seem to be the equivalent of a witchy sponge, soaking up all kinds of random knowledge about Salem and the witches who lived here.

But maybe Grace would also want to put the kibosh on my explorations. That was part of the problem of being one of the youngest witches in the coven—even though I was supposed to have equal rights and an equal say, the older witches always seemed far too ready to tell me all the reasons why I shouldn't do something.

In which case, it was probably smarter to stay quiet.

After about fifteen minutes or so, I called to Lionel and Milo so they could come inside and have their dinners. While they ate, I engaged in some minor primping to get ready for my date with Noah, then told the two of them I would be going over to his house.

"But I won't be late," I said...not bothering to mention that I didn't intend to come straight home after the barbecue.

No, I had another date, this one with that mysterious passageway in my shop's basement.

Both the familiars seemed just fine with my plan, especially after I reassured them once again that I'd be home well before ten.

"You should have Noah come over here next time, though," Milo said. "I miss him."

I patted the dog on the head. "That can be arranged. Anyway, you two be good. I'll be home before you know it."

As I pulled out of the driveway, though, I couldn't help wondering if I'd just made a promise I might not be able to keep.

Chapter 11

Face to Face

"CAN YOU THINK OF A REASON WHY someone would lie about where they were going on their honeymoon?" I asked Noah after bringing him up to date on what I'd learned from Derek Falco.

Noah had just taken a bite of his hamburger when I made the inquiry, so I had to wait for him to finish chewing before he could respond. "I'm not sure," he said. "My first thought would be that Sela Warren was being secretive because her family was against the marriage, but it doesn't sound like that's what's going on here."

No, it couldn't be, not when it seemed as though Anna had been Sela's only living relative, and, from what Maggie had told me, it sounded as if Anna had been happy that her sister was happy.

What if she'd just been pretending, though?

What if there were sour grapes involved? After all, some women might have been jealous to have a younger sister find happiness with a handsome doctor when they themselves were obviously single...happily so, according to Tonya, but people often put on a public face to hide what was actually going on inside.

Even if there had been some animosity between the Warren sisters, though, that didn't explain the hex that had caused Anna's aneurysm. No, something else was going on here.

"How much do you know about this Colin person?" Noah asked then, and I found myself shrugging.

"Not a lot," I replied. "What Maggie Phillips told me, of course, and then I looked up his bio on the hospital's website. It was pretty much all the same information, though. If he's on social media, he must not post at all, because I couldn't find anything."

"That doesn't surprise me," Noah said. "People in the medical profession tend to keep their profiles pretty locked down because they don't want patients looking up personal information about them. I don't even have any social media accounts except the one for the clinic, and that's a business page, not a personal profile."

Right. I had to admit that when I first brought a familiar to be seen by Noah Jenkins a little over a year ago, I'd tried doing a little internet sleuthing just to see if I could find out something about the handsome vet...like if he had a wife.

But there was only the Facebook page for the clinic, and an Instagram account attached to the page, an account that seemed to exist solely to post information about pet adoptions in the area or highlight that it was national spay or neuter your pet day, that kind of stuff. There definitely wasn't any personal information to be gleaned from it.

"I don't think there's anything nefarious going on with Colin Novak, though," I remarked. "Maggie made it seem as if he's a pretty stand-up guy. I get the feeling all this secrecy was Sela's idea, and he went along with it just because he could tell it was important to her."

"Maybe," Noah said. "But because finding out anything more about Sela and her sister seems like kind of a dead end, you might want to focus your efforts on Colin and his own family and friends. One of them might let slip exactly the kind of information you've been looking for."

This was such a piece of sound advice that I wanted to kick myself for not following up on it earlier. Maybe Detective Finley had already been in touch with a bunch of people in Colin's circle and hadn't found anything valuable.

Or maybe he hadn't bothered, since this was all way beyond the scope of the routine investigation into Anna Warren's death, the sort of thing that always happened when an otherwise healthy person dropped dead for no reason. No one had reported Colin as a missing person, and obviously no one had bothered to do that in Sela's case, either.

Because there's no one left to report her missing, I thought, the realization bringing on a sense of melancholy. It was kind of awful to think she didn't have anyone at all besides her business partner.

Well, no one except the man she'd just married.

Who I knew next to nothing about.

"I'll do that," I said. Maybe it would be better to postpone my exploration of the passageway in the shop basement until later, once I'd tried to find out more about Colin Novak. After all, that tunnel wasn't going anywhere.

And I had to admit I wasn't terribly eager to go down there. What if there were more rats?

Or bats...or centipedes...or....

I managed to hold back a shudder. The last thing I wanted was for Noah to ask any probing questions. No, I wanted him to think I was concentrating on Colin and nothing else.

Here's hoping it would be worth it.

～

However, when I came back to the shop the next morning, I still brought along some sneakers, a compass, and a higher-powered flashlight than the one I kept in the basement, my rationale being that there was a strong possibility there wouldn't be very much to discover about Colin Novak, and I'd have time at the end of the day to go exploring after all.

I also brought my laptop, since it would be a lot easier to do some heavy-duty sleuthing on that rather than my phone. The phone would still come in useful, since I'd have to use it as a wi-fi hotspot— the store didn't have its own wi-fi, as I'd decided a while back that I didn't want to bother with it, and instead used a dedicated phone line for my credit card processing.

Anyway, I put the laptop on the little table in the back that functioned as a break area for the times I couldn't get away for lunch, and was working there when Sage appeared at about a quarter to ten.

"Doing homework?" she asked with a grin.

"Sort of," I replied. "I'm trying to see if I can find out anything about Colin Novak, the man Sela Warren married. I know he's a doctor at the children's hospital over in Peabody, but that's about it."

Sage nodded, a knowing expression spreading

across her face. "Got it. Well, I'll keep an eye on things out front. If it gets too crazy, I'll yell."

"Thanks," I said, and meant it. It wasn't my intention to completely shirk my shopkeeping duties, but if Sage could take care of handling customers until we really got busy, I'd probably get a lot more done.

Luckily, Colin Novak had a last name that wasn't very common in our area, one that shouldn't be too hard to track across social media. In fact, I hit pay dirt on Facebook right away—his mother had a chatty account there that didn't seem to be locked down at all, and it sounded as if she still lived in Marblehead, in the big Colonial-style house where he and his two younger sisters had grown up.

In fact, there was a picture of the happy couple themselves, in a photo that looked like it had been taken on the patio at one of the restaurants near the harbor. The sun was shining brightly, so Colin and Sela were both wearing sunglasses, and they held what I guessed were pints of beer or hard cider. They were smiling broadly, and since they were both very attractive, they honestly looked like a couple you'd find in one of those placeholder images companies always put in photo frames to make them appear more appealing.

Big News! the post under the photo said, and proclaimed to the world that Colin Novak and Sela

Warren had just gotten engaged. The post's date stamp was Tuesday, June thirteenth, which made me frown a little, wondering.

Had Sela been so eager to leave town because that unwitting post had let the proverbial cat out of the bag regarding her engagement to Colin?

No date yet, Colin's mother, Barri, had added. *But we'll let you all know as soon as we know.*

I didn't see any posts referencing a wedding after that, though. Did Barri Novak and her husband even know that their son had eloped, or did they just think that Colin and Sela had gone on vacation together?

There was a question...and not the sort of thing I could exactly bring up in a random Facebook comment.

However, the bio on her profile said that she and her husband were the owners of the Driftwood Tavern, probably the very place where that photo of Sela and Colin had been taken. It wouldn't take me very long to nip over to Marblehead and see if Barri was working there, especially since I got the impression she was the kind of hands-on business owner who liked to be present most of the time rather than leaving all the day-to-day stuff to a manager.

And if she wasn't there, well, I'd ask around and see if anyone knew where I might find her.

"Hey, Sage," I said, after I'd gotten up from

where I'd been sitting with my laptop and headed to the front of the store.

She raised an amused eyebrow. "Let me guess— you just found a clue you need to go track down."

"You got me," I said. Considering how many times I'd run off to deal with Milo's dognapping a few weeks ago—and how often I'd had to beg off from work so I could help figure out who had really killed Shelby Howard's ex-fiancé—I supposed it wasn't too strange that Sage had guessed exactly what I was up to now. "I need to go over to Marblehead for a bit...unless you think it's going to be too busy here. Then this can probably wait for a while."

At least, I hoped it would. It seemed as if I had a slightly better chance of finding Barri Novak in the middle of the day, rather than on a Friday night, but....

"It's fine," Sage said. "I mean, it's not like it's been dead here today, but I can manage. Go track down your clue."

"Thanks," I told her, then hurried to the back of the shop so I could grab my purse and unhook my phone from my laptop, although I left the computer there.

A minute later, I was backing out from my parking space at the rear of the shop and heading down to Canal Street, which would lead me out of Salem and southeast toward Marblehead. It would be a little after eleven by the time I got there, and I hoped I wasn't jumping the gun, that I wouldn't get all the way to the restaurant the Novaks owned, only to find out they didn't open until later in the day.

But no, the door to the Driftwood Tavern was open when I got there, probably to let in the fresh breeze off the ocean. It was a cute place, painted white with bright blue shutters, very clean and nautical-looking.

And there was Barri Novak, wiping down the bar as I walked in. At that hour of the day, there wasn't anyone in that part of the restaurant, although I'd spied a large family group occupying the patio as I walked past, obviously wanting to enjoy the beautiful day.

In person, Barri looked just as cheerful as she had in her Facebook profile photo, an attractive woman around my mother's age or maybe a little older, with wavy light brown hair cut in a chin-length bob and bright blue eyes. The resemblance to her son was strong; it seemed pretty obvious to me that he must take after her much more than he did his father.

Barri greeted me as I sat down at the bar. "What can I get for you?"

"An iced tea, please."

She fetched a glass from the stack to one side of the serving area, poured some tea out of a pitcher, and pushed it across the bar-top toward me. "Would you like a straw?"

"Yes, please."

A pause as she got one out of the dispenser on the counter behind her. "There you go."

I thanked her again, then ventured, "Are you Barri Novak?"

"I am," she replied. "Did you find me on Facebook?"

"I did," I said, a little startled. However, her meaning became clearer when she continued.

"My husband thinks it's silly for me to have our photos on the page for the restaurant, but I think it gives the place a nice, personal touch. This way, people know who they're working with when they come in. Your first time here?"

I nodded. "I actually live in Salem, but I don't get over to Marblehead much."

Which wasn't exactly the truth...we came here to go to the brewery because Noah really liked it, but I hadn't visited the harbor more than a couple of times. It was also pretty touristy, and since I worked five days a week in a store in the heart of Salem's most-visited section, I tended to avoid places like that when I could.

"But I know a few people from here," I went on. "Like Sela Warren. You know her?"

At once, Barri Novak's face brightened. "Oh, yes. A lovely girl. She and my son just got engaged."

"Wow," I said, hoping I sounded sufficiently surprised. "I hadn't heard that, but it's been a while since Sela and I spoke. Congratulations!"

Still beaming, Barri replied, "The whole family is thrilled for them. In fact, they're both off on an engagement trip to Cancun."

Praying that my expression hadn't shifted, I said, "That sounds like fun."

"It's just what Colin needed," Barri told me. "He's been working so hard the past couple of years, ever since his marriage broke up." Voice lowering, she went on, "Just between you and me, I never thought he and Maureen were a very good match, so I wasn't too upset when they decided to split."

It sure seemed like Barri in person didn't have any more of a filter than her Facebook persona did. Which was great for me—even though it appeared as though she didn't have any more of a clue than anyone else as to exactly what her son was up to, it still meant I'd be able to get some helpful information from her about his and Sela's relationship.

"Some people might think that Colin and Sela got serious too fast," Barri said. "But I just think that when you know, you know, right?"

"Right," I echoed, and took a sip of my iced tea. "So...they hadn't been seeing each other for very long before they got engaged?"

"Only a month. But I knew it was serious right

away, because after their first date, Colin called me to say he'd met someone special and that he thought she might actually be the one." Barri's expression turned dreamy, and she added, "It was like that when I met Colin's father, so I knew exactly what he meant. And after Colin's breakup from Maureen, I started to wonder if he'd ever be interested in dating again. His sisters are both happily married and have started their families, and I wanted the same thing for Colin, too."

"Have you heard anything from him?" I asked. "I mean, to let you know how his trip is going."

To my relief, Barri didn't appear to see anything strange about my asking such a personal question. "Oh, yes," she replied at once. "He's texted a couple of times. He apologized for not sending any photos, but I guess something wonky is going on with his phone's camera. But he said he's having a great time."

From the sound of it, Colin seemed just as invested in hiding his true destination—and his reason for being there—from the world as Sela, although at least he'd taken the step of staying in touch with his mother so she'd know everything was okay.

And since he'd been communicating with Barri, that told me the newlyweds were alive and well, just doing their best to hide their location from everyone else.

Well, unless someone has done away with them and is using Colin's phone to make his family think they're still alive, passed through my brain, although I did my best to brush aside the ugly thought. While there was definitely some weirdness going on here, I didn't think it quite rose to that level.

I hoped.

"I'm glad," I said. "I haven't talked to Sela lately, but I know she's been working hard, and it sounds as if both she and Colin definitely deserved a vacation."

"Oh, they did," Barri responded. "She and her business partner have really expanded the business lately—I think they just got a big contract with a local hotel—and they've been putting in a lot of hours. Honestly, if Colin hadn't come and told me they planned to go to Cancun, I would have said he needed a vacation, stat."

She looked very proud of her doctor son as she made that comment, and I supposed she should be. From everything I'd heard, he seemed like a nice man, and someone who deserved a little happiness in his life.

I just hoped his happiness hadn't come at a cost he shouldn't have to pay.

"How's your tea?" Barri asked next, as if realizing she was also supposed to be acting the role of hostess here.

"Great," I said, which was the truth. It was just strong enough to have some personality without knocking me over with caffeine.

"Did you want to have lunch?" she went on. "I can get you a menu."

"No, thank you," I replied quickly. I had no reason to believe the food here wasn't as good as the iced tea, but I'd picked up some valuable information and knew I needed to be getting back to the store. "I was actually just running an errand here in town and stopped in because I was thirsty, but I need to get going. How much do I owe you for the tea?"

"Two fifty," she said. Her expression told me she was a little disappointed that I wasn't staying for lunch, but at least she didn't press me.

I fished a five-dollar bill out of my wallet and gave it to her. "Thanks so much for the tea—and the conversation."

She gave me an uncertain smile, as if realizing for the first time that maybe I had more of a reason for visiting her than running some nebulous "errand." To my relief, though, she didn't ask any uncomfortable questions, but instead got some change out of the cash register and began to hand it to me.

"No, keep it," I said quickly. "You have a good rest of your day."

Before she could protest, I slid off the barstool

and hurried to the door, then emerged into the bright midday sunlight. Immediately, I got my sunglasses out of my purse and planted them on my nose, and walked over to the place where I'd left my SUV in the parking lot.

Barri Novak had told me a lot...but I still was no closer to figuring out why Sela and Colin were so determined to hide their location from the rest of the world than I'd been when I set out on this errand.

Well, at least you know they're alive, I thought as I started the Discovery's engine.

...if that was even true.

Chapter 12

Gone to Ground

THE ENTIRE TRIP HAD ONLY TAKEN ME AN hour, and when I got back to the shop, I told Sage to go ahead and have her lunch break. She didn't ask me what I'd been up to, only said she'd be back in half an hour and asked if I wanted anything from the sandwich store.

A sandwich sounded like a good idea, so I said I'd love a roast beef and provolone, and handed her a ten-dollar bill. Once she was gone, though, I found myself frowning.

Barri Novak appeared to have taken everything her son told her at face value, but didn't she think it was kind of strange that the couple hadn't sent her any photos at all of their vacation? Yes, Colin had obviously been lying when he said his phone's camera was acting up, but if I'd been in Barri's position, I would have simply asked whether Sela could have sent me some pictures.

Then again, I was clearly a much more suspicious person than Barri Novak could ever hope to be.

All right, at least it had been established that Colin's family definitely liked Sela, so it wasn't as though they'd eloped because they thought someone would try to stop them. True, one could also argue that a pair of grown-ups didn't need anyone else's approval to get married, but I knew families could sometimes get very weird about that kind of thing. Barri hadn't even seemed too put off by how quickly the couple had gotten engaged, which surprised me somewhat. In my own case, my mother was thrilled that I was dating Noah, but even she would have a few choice words to say on the subject if I went to her and announced we were getting married after only dating for a month.

So, what I had now were a few more pieces of information that still didn't seem to add up to anything useful. About all I could do was file them away and hope that at some later date, they'd begin to make sense.

Well, at the rate you're going, you won't find anything before Sela and Colin get back, and you can ask her then, I thought sourly.

If they came back.

I tried to ignore that pessimistic thought and instead told myself I still had the passageway to investigate. Not that I believed it had anything to do with Sela and Colin's disappearing act—or Anna Warren's tragic death—but at least wandering around in the tunnels underneath Salem would be a good way to distract myself. Noah and I didn't have plans tonight, because he was performing surgery tomorrow morning at seven o'clock, a concession to the dog's owner, who had to be at work at nine and couldn't move his schedule around.

Which meant I was absolutely free to do whatever I wanted this evening. Yes, I couldn't exactly abandon Milo and Lionel, but I'd already decided that I would go home and feed them first, then come back and start my explorations. Because I sometimes came into the shop after hours if I had a lot of inventory to do—or was dropping off a batch of elixirs and philters I'd just brewed—no one would think it too strange if they saw my Land Rover parked out back.

Although business picked up in the middle of the afternoon, I still found myself restless, wishing the day would be over so I could go explore the tunnel. Maybe I wouldn't find anything at all, but it was still something novel to investigate, and I felt like I definitely needed a break from beating my head against the wall with this whole Sela Warren problem.

The two familiars didn't seem too upset when I told them I'd be heading out again this evening, although I promised them I wouldn't be late.

"This'll probably only take an hour at the most," I said. "But I've turned on the lights in the kitchen and the living room, just in case."

Milo nodded, while Lionel stood a foot or so away from him, his expression solemn.

"What are you doing at the shop?" the dog asked.

For a moment, I hesitated, wondering if I should try to hedge and say something non-specific. But Milo—and Lionel—deserved the truth. Besides, it wasn't as though I expected them to try to stop me.

"I found a passageway in the storage area in the basement," I said. "It probably connects to the tunnels under Salem Common and that area, but I figured I might as well check it out. I'm sure it's perfectly safe."

Milo didn't look too convinced by that argument. "Are you sure? A tunnel sounds like it could lead to all sorts of scary stuff."

"Really, it's fine," I assured him. "People take tours through those tunnels all the time. I just didn't realize they extended as far as the shop. As soon as I figure out if the one at the store connects to the smugglers' tunnels, I'll turn around and come back."

And then make plans to have the passageway sealed up again. Hidden tunnels were all well and good, but if the people leading those tours decided to go exploring a little further, I really didn't want them barging into my storage room without any notice.

My explanation must have made sense to Milo, because he didn't offer any further protests, and only nodded, brown floppy ears bouncing a little as he did so.

"That seems safe," he said. "I didn't realize people went in those tunnels."

"All the time," I replied. I'd never gone on one of those tours, but I'd read about them, and I had to assume I would have heard something if there had ever been any incidents involving the tourists or their guides.

With all those reassurances out of the way, I headed outside and got in my SUV, which I'd left in the driveway rather than parking it in the garage. Despite the calming words I'd spoken to Milo and Lionel, I couldn't quite ignore the shiver of unease that moved down my spine. Maybe the main parts of those tunnels were completely safe, but they were also blocks away from my shop. Anything could lie between here and there.

Or there could be nothing at all except a few

hundred yards of hollowed-out earth, maybe with a few spiders and rats to add some extra excitement. All the same, it would be good to learn where that tunnel went.

I parked in my usual space behind the shop and went in. Even though I came here after hours from time to time, this particular evening, it still felt strange to be there, everything dark and silent. At once, my hand went to the light switch immediately inside the back door, and I flicked on the fluorescents overhead.

There, that was a little better.

After I set my purse on the table in the break area, I got out the flashlight I'd tucked in there a while earlier. I'd already changed into my sneakers, so there wasn't much left for me to do except head to the stairs that led to the basement, turning on lights as I went.

The same gaping hole in the cellar wall awaited me, although I didn't know what else I'd been expecting to find. For a long moment, I stood in front of it, asking myself for what felt like the hundredth time whether this really was a good idea after all.

The sooner you go, the sooner you'll come back, I reminded myself.

That seemed to do it. I switched on the flashlight, took a bracing breath, and stepped inside the passageway.

Almost at once, the temperature seemed to drop, even though I told myself that had to be my imagination, since the tunnel wasn't any deeper in the ground than the basement, and it wasn't as if I'd been running a heater in there or something. All the same, I found myself shivering again, and wished I'd put on a sweatshirt or at least something warmer than the sleeveless top I was currently wearing.

Since there wasn't much I could do about it now, I only tightened my grip on the flashlight and kept going.

To tell the truth, there really wasn't all that much to see. The walls in this section of the passageway seemed to be bare dirt, although I noticed they were braced with old, old timber, some of it beginning to rot in certain places.

Honestly, I was kind of surprised the whole thing hadn't collapsed over the years.

I'd never been very good at measuring distance, so I wasn't sure how far I'd gone before I came to a branch in the tunnel. Pausing, I got a compass out of my jeans pocket, where I'd stowed it before leaving the house, and shone the flashlight on its face. Right now I was facing south, and the tunnel formed a T-intersection here.

East or west. Which would it be?

Since my gut didn't seem interested in making a decision, I figured it didn't matter so much.

All right, east it was.

Before I took another step, though, I returned the compass to my pocket, placed a hand on the tunnel wall next to me, and cast a quick spell.

Earth and stone, bind this place tight,
Mark it well, in day or night,
Guide my steps, no matter the cost,
May I find my way and not be lost.

At least this way, if I left little glowing bread-crumbs behind me, I'd be able to find my way back without too much trouble. I was taking a little risk, because if anyone who led the Salem Underground tours came along this particular tunnel, they'd be sure to see those markers. However, since it really just looked as if someone had marked the spot with glow-in-the-dark paint, I was all right with taking that chance.

As I headed east—well, south and east, according to my compass—the ground beneath my feet changed, wasn't packed dirt any longer, but actual stone, worn as if plenty of people had gone this way over the years. And the walls were also much more finished, appeared to be shored up with nicely set bricks rather than the haphazard mix of old bricks and stone I'd seen in the passage next to the store's basement.

Had I already reached the section of the tunnels that passed underneath the old town square?

That didn't seem right, though. The passageway that opened up off my cellar had pointed pretty much due south, away from Essex Street, not north and west where the Commons were located. I was going in almost the opposite direction from where I should have been.

Well, just because the tour companies operated in one specific area, that didn't mean there couldn't be more tunnels crisscrossing their way beneath the town. Salem was an ancient place by U.S. standards, and although the settlement had been thoroughly researched and documented, that didn't mean the old girl didn't still have some secrets left in her.

After walking for a few more minutes, I came to another crossroads, this one with new tunnels branching in all four directions. Should I keep going the way I had been, or should I try an alternative path?

I really didn't know. Right then, I realized that this little expedition wasn't as straightforward as I'd thought it would be, that I could wander around down here for hours and hours if I wanted to. The smart thing to do would be to go back the way I'd come, head for home...and call my contractor the next morning so he could come out and patch that gaping hole in my basement.

Naturally, I wasn't about to do that. I did, however, magically mark the wall again, this time with an obvious arrow so I'd know which was the way back to the original passage off the store's cellar. As for which direction to head now, I thought I might as well keep on keeping on.

Too bad I didn't have a Fitbit or something similar, just so I could keep track of how many steps I'd taken. I paused to pull my phone out of my other pocket and look down at the screen. It showed a distressing lack of bars, but at least I could see it was still pretty early, not even seven o'clock yet. My promise to Milo and Lionel that I wouldn't be out very late looked like one I'd be able to keep.

Slightly reassured, I kept walking.

And walking...and walking.

The farther you go, the longer it'll take to get back, I warned myself.

True, although I had the feeling part of the reason I didn't turn around was that I kept hoping to see something of note, something that would tell me why these tunnels existed in the first place. And okay, I knew smugglers had built them centuries ago and the original reason for their construction no longer even existed, but I had to believe someone was using them now, or they wouldn't be in such good repair.

I pulled out my phone again.

7:56.

So, I'd been walking for nearly an hour—and walking at a good clip, which meant I might have already covered a mile or more.

Did the tunnels really extend that far?

It sure looked as though they did. If I'd walked more than a mile, then that meant I must have gone right under the college and was now near the southeast edge of Salem's town limits, almost to the border we shared with Marblehead.

What would be the point in going any farther? I hadn't found a single thing of note down here, except the obvious fact that this tunnel system was much larger and more complicated than I'd previously thought. And even though it probably wouldn't make any difference one way or another, something felt wrong about leaving Salem and going into the neighboring town, even though I'd done that very thing earlier today.

All right, that seemed to decide things.

I reached out to touch the wall, figuring I'd leave another glowing marker here to show where I'd stopped walking—even though the spells had a finite duration, and they wouldn't last more than twenty-four hours—only to have a woman with

long white hair and wearing a black dress materi-
alize in the middle of the tunnel a few feet away.

The strange witch...I knew I'd never seen her
before...shot me a malevolent smile.

"Trespassing, I see," she said, and before I could
even begin to react, she lifted her hands and
muttered a quick spell under her breath.

The last thing I saw before everything went
black was the glitter of her pale blue eyes and the
gleam of her white teeth as she leaned over me, still
wearing that evil smile.

I woke up in a sitting position. The chair where I
sat was a comfortable one, soft velvet with well-
padded arms and an equally accommodating seat
cushion.

What wasn't so comfortable was the spell
holding me in place, something that felt like ropes
but was completely invisible.

Standing in front of me was a group of six
witches, ranging in age from what I guessed was
their early or mid-sixties, all the way down to one
blonde girl who didn't look much older than Sage.
They all wore the same stern, disapproving expres-
sions, though, telling me that even though they
were disparate in age, they definitely seemed to be

of the same mind when it came to my presence in their territory.

I thought I even recognized a couple of the women, probably because they'd come to my shop from time to time to buy arthritis tinctures and insomnia elixirs, although I couldn't have called them out by name.

"What were you doing in our tunnels?" the oldest witch, the white-haired one who'd first confronted me, demanded.

"*Your* tunnels?" I responded. Although fear was a tightly coiled knot in the pit of my stomach, I refused to give in to it. For one thing, if they'd really meant me any harm, I didn't think they would have bound me in this comfy chair, and second, it was hard to look at fellow witches as my enemy. True, witches in their individual towns tended to stick close to home, but that didn't mean we couldn't come and go as we pleased. "I figured they belonged to everybody—you know, like a public highway."

The older witch exchanged a sour glance with the woman standing next to her, who looked as though she was in her late forties or early fifties, with dark hair braided away from her face and a couple of stray gray strands showing near her temples.

"There's nothing public about it," the younger of the two said, and the rest of their little group murmured agreement. "You crossed into the Marblehead side and set off our alarms."

I hadn't heard anything, but I supposed that was the point. It wasn't too hard to cast a spell that would alert you when someone outside your coven blundered into a space you wanted kept private. Marblehead was smaller than Salem by a good bit, and only had two or three covens rather than Salem's six or so—the witch population in my hometown was much higher than average because witches came there to enjoy the relative openness with which we lived our lives—and therefore that kind of alarm setup made some sense.

Or at least, it made sense if you were willing to admit that a particular coven might be up to a whole lot of no good. None of the women here were witches I knew personally, unlike Hester, the Marblehead-based lactation coach I'd helped by creating a milk-producing potion...the same thing I'd brewed for Cinny, the cat familiar who wanted to be a mother...or Meadow, the witch who'd been in several of my psych classes at Salem State University.

Come to think of it, Hester and Meadow were both in the same coven.

Did they know any of these women? Probably; Marblehead wasn't a very big town. However, I had a feeling that Meadow and Hester—and the rough dozen or so other witches who lived there—

had no idea that the magical practitioners who stood in front of me now might be up to no good.

"Kidnapping is illegal, whether you're a witch or not," I said, a little surprised by my boldness. "I'm pretty sure the police would be much more interested in that than a possible case of trespassing."

The white-haired witch gave me a thin smile. "Well, that's only if they find out about it."

My stomach tightened, but since I'd already started acting tough, I couldn't exactly back down now. "So...what? You're going to kill me?"

Her smile stretched a little further. "Oh, that's not necessary. Just a minor spell, one to make you forget you were ever here, that anything more happened than tripping and falling in the tunnel, and knocking yourself unconscious. The ground in there is awfully uneven, after all."

To my surprise, she nodded toward the pretty blonde witch, the one who looked barely old enough to drink. "Lily, go ahead and take care of our problem, would you?"

Lily stepped forward. Unlike the others, she wasn't smiling, but she didn't look particularly sympathetic, either. No, her expression was closer to the one you might wear when you were trying to remember a bunch of trig formulas right before taking a final.

· · ·

Memories fade, let time unwind,
Erase the truth from heart and mind,
With whispered words, her thoughts I sway,
The incriminating sight, now fade away,
Innocence restored, secrets sealed,
Let forgetfulness be her shield.

And everything went black.

Chapter 13

Trip Down Memory Lane

I SAT UP IN THE DARKNESS AND PUT A HAND to my forehead. My exploring fingers felt a definite bump, telling me I was lucky I'd only knocked myself out instead of splattering my brains all over the walls of the tunnel.

A few feet away lay my flashlight. I must have dropped it when I fell, but because I couldn't remember exactly what had happened—the whole incident felt foggy and hazy, like something from a dream that began slipping away the moment I opened my eyes—I couldn't know for sure.

What I did know was that I ached all over, and when I staggered to my feet, the tunnel spun around me for a couple of dizzying seconds. I put a hand on the wall to steady myself, and that helped a little. I stood like that for a moment or two, wanting to make sure I wasn't going to go *ker-splat* as soon as I tried to put one foot in front of the other.

Once the spinning stopped, I gingerly made my way over to pick up the flashlight, knowing I'd never find my way back to the shop's basement without it. As I hefted it in one hand, the beam passed over a piece of broken flagstone sticking up from the ground.

Well, I seemed to have found the culprit.

I gave the stone as wide a berth as possible as I began to stumble along the tunnel, pausing every once in a while to hold the wall again whenever one of those awful dizzy spells attacked. Eventually, though, they seemed to go away altogether, although I was still careful about where I stepped, and shone the flashlight back and forth across the ground as I went.

Another spill like that might have left me lying unconscious for hours.

Because I was moving so slowly, the return trip seemed to take forever. I didn't lose my way, though, thanks to the glowing little marks I'd left on the walls to guide me back to the store.

Not going to lie—when I finally spied the irregular hole that opened into the basement, I let out a little sob of relief. Even though my logical side had known it wasn't going to happen, some-thing irrational deep inside had been worried that I'd arrive there and find the opening into the cellar gone and I'd be forced to wander these tunnels forever.

Even if something so improbable had happened, all I would have had to do was take the branch to the right, which would lead me to the part of the network that the Salem Underground people included in their tours. Someone would have found me eventually.

But I'd discovered that my brain didn't always function as its usual rational self when I was roaming through the bowels of the earth. That was okay, though—I had no intention of ever going back down there. Tomorrow morning, I'd be on the phone to the same contractor who'd fixed my leaky roof and installed my new windows, and I'd see if he could take care of patching that hole.

Once I was safely back in the basement, I pulled out my phone.

11:52.

Had I really been roaming around in the tunnels for the greater part of six hours? It didn't feel like it, but then again, I had no idea how long I'd been knocked out. I supposed I should just be glad that I hadn't smashed my phone when I fell.

Milo and Lionel must have been frantic by now, which meant I needed to get the hell out of here and head for home.

I went over to the stairs, turned off the lights, and laboriously made my way up to the shop's main floor. As I went, muscles I hadn't used recently twinged with fresh pain.

That must have been some fall.

But I was safe now, and that was the important thing.

I turned on the store's alarm, locked the door, and climbed into my Discovery. That hurt as well, and I found myself thinking maybe it would have been smarter to get a nice, low-slung sedan like a Camry or an Accord instead of such a tall SUV.

Since I couldn't do anything about that now, I gritted my teeth as I buckled the seatbelt, then backed out of my parking space. At this hour, Salem's streets were quiet, nearly deserted. A good thing, since I drove much faster than I should have on my way home, mostly because all I wanted to do was fall into bed.

Well, after dragging myself up the stairs, of course. Yes, I ached all over, but I had to hope most of those aches and pains would get better after a decent night's sleep. I wasn't in bad enough shape to go to the emergency room, and we didn't have a twenty-four-hour urgent care here in town. And while the witches in my coven were all talented in their various ways, none of them were healers.

Milo was waiting for me at the back door, furry forehead crinkled in concern.

"You're really late," he said after I closed the door behind me and locked it.

"I know," I replied. "I had a little accident."

At once, he came up to me and sniffed my hand. "You smell like underground. What happened?"

"I tripped and fell," I said. "But I'm okay now."

Mostly okay, anyway. I still hurt all over, but my head wasn't aching as much, telling me I didn't have a concussion.

Hopefully.

"I knew I should have gone with you," Milo said, and now his tone was reproachful, although I guessed most of that was him chiding himself for not insisting on coming along on my little expedition.

"No, it was better for you to stay here with Lionel," I returned, and glanced down the hallway toward the living room, where I presumed the hedgehog was sleeping in his basket. "Is he okay?"

"He's fine," Milo said. "The hex is definitely gone."

Well, that was something.

"I'm dead tired, though," I went on. "And I have to be at work tomorrow. So I'm going to drag myself upstairs and go to sleep. Can you stay down here with Lionel?"

"You're not sleeping by yourself, not after you fell," Milo told me, in tones that brooked no argument. "I can get Lionel. Just wait a second."

Before I could say anything to stop him, he

bounded down the hallway to the living room, then returned a moment later with Lionel's basket hanging from between his teeth. It was too big for him to carry and in real danger of scraping against the floor, so I took it from him, trying to convince myself that it wouldn't require too much effort for me to go up the steps and hold the basket at the same time.

Somehow, I managed the feat, although I felt as if I was attempting to scale Mount Everest, not climb up an ordinary set of stairs. Eventually, though, I reached the landing at the top and stumbled into my bedroom.

I wasn't so out of it that I dropped the basket, even if it ended up landing on my dresser with a little more force than I would have liked.

At once, Lionel poked his pointed, pixie-ish face out from inside the basket. "I was asleep, you know."

"Sorry about that," I replied automatically, even as I was amazed that he'd managed to sleep all the way through Milo picking him up and me carrying him upstairs, and had only been awakened when I put the basket on the dresser. "But we're all going to sleep now."

The hedgehog glanced over at Milo, who nodded, as if to reassure the little creature that it really was lights out at the Hughes household at last.

I was so tired that I didn't even bother to go into the bathroom to wash my face and brush my teeth, and instead only pulled off my sneakers and clothes, and climbed into my bed wearing my underwear and nothing else.

This day couldn't end soon enough for me.

The alarm woke me up, which it hardly ever did. Groggily, I reached over to shut it off...and only succeeded in knocking the clock onto the floor.

Goddamn it.

Milo had startled awake as soon as the alarm clock landed on the rug. After I set it back in its place on the nightstand, he cocked his head, looking almost but not quite accusatory.

"I don't think you're in any shape to go to work today."

There was an understatement. If possible, I hurt even worse than I had the day before, and when I staggered out of bed and went into the bathroom to splash some cold water on my face, it was only to find that I had a lovely little bluish-purple marble of a bruise rising in the center of my forehead, like I was about to start sprouting a horn or something.

That's why God invented foundation, I told myself.

Barring that, maybe it was time to think about getting some bangs.

However, even if I was able to physically cover up the evidence of my fall from the night before, it wouldn't do anything to fix the way I felt.

Well, I didn't have to be at work for almost three hours. Maybe some coffee and breakfast would improve my outlook on life.

After consuming two cups of coffee and two slices of sourdough toast with fresh strawberry preserves, I didn't feel quite as much like the walking dead, but I also wasn't sure whether I was ready to face a store full of customers for the next eight hours. If it had been a quiet weekday, I might have risked going in anyway, but the mere thought of dealing with Saturday crowds only made my head start hurting all over again.

I went ahead and showered and got dressed, and that helped a little, too. On the other hand, I still didn't feel like doing anything except putting my feet up on the sofa and binge-watching an entire season of *The $100,000 Pyramid* on the small TV from the guest bedroom, which I'd brought into the living room a few days back.

That seemed to settle things. I got out my phone and sent Sage a quick text.

I'm really feeling like crap today. Do you want to keep the shop closed, or do you think you could handle it on your own?

Her reply came back so quickly, I guessed she must have already been on her phone for some other reason.

I can handle it. Do you want me to come over & get the key?

Yes, please.

Thank God for Sage. I would never have flat-out told her she had to man the store by herself, but if she thought she could do it, at least I wouldn't have to close up shop on what was usually my busiest sales day.

She came over and knocked on the front door, took one look at the bruise on my forehead, and exclaimed, "What happened?"

"I fell," I told her. "It's not as bad as it looks, but I still want to take it easy today."

"I get it," she said. "The key?"

Oh, right. I dug it out of my pocket and handed it over, and she said she'd come by around five-thirty to drop it off at the end of the day.

That seemed to be that. But even though I thought it had been a good idea to stay home, once I realized I had the entire day ahead of me, I wasn't sure what to do with myself. Working in the garden didn't seem like a very good idea, but my industrious Virgo nature really didn't like the idea of lying around and watching TV, either.

You're supposed to rest, I scolded myself. *Then rest, dammit.*

So I made myself a cup of peppermint tea, and headed into the living room to drink it and allow myself to relax for a while. Once I was done with the tea, then I could decide if I felt up to anything more physical than sitting on the sofa with my feet up.

I hadn't even taken my first sip before my phone *binged*, letting me know I had a text message.

Noah? I really hadn't expected to hear from him this morning, since he had an early surgery and would be busy. And obviously, he would have no reason to believe I wasn't doing anything except working a regular day.

But the message wasn't from Noah.

It was from Sela.

I know I'm supposed to pick up Lionel tomorrow, but I won't be able to make it. Will try to be there next week sometime.

My head fairly spun. So, ten days of no contact, and then she just casually texts me to let me know she wouldn't be coming home when she was supposed to?

Fingers flying, I flung back a text of my own.

You need to come home. It's important.

I know what happened. But I can't come yet.

Why not?

I can't tell you that. I'll try to be back sometime next week.

She knew what had happened to Anna, and she still intended to stay away?

None of this made any sense.

What happens if you don't come back?

I'll be back. It's a matter of when, not if.

And even though we were exchanging text messages, it pretty much felt as though she'd just hung up the phone on me. I had no doubt that if I tried to message her again, the only response I'd get was dead silence.

"I can't come yet."

What the hell was that supposed to mean? What force in the world could possibly be keeping her away, especially if she knew that her sister had died while she was out of the country?

I wondered how she'd found out. Had Barri Novak said something to her son? If that was the case, why hadn't Barri held Colin's feet to the fire and told him he and Sela needed to come home immediately?

Maybe she had. And maybe he'd said no. I couldn't begin to understand what justification he possibly could have provided that would have explained why it was all right for Sela to remain on vacation after discovering her sister had just died.

Not for the first time, I thought that none of this made any damn sense.

Because there wasn't much else I could do, I sipped some of my peppermint tea. Milo and

Lionel were out in the backyard, getting their fill of the bright early-morning sunshine, both of them obviously glad that I had stayed home and wouldn't be leaving them to fend for themselves while I was at work.

What in the world would Lionel think when I told him I didn't know when his mistress would be coming home?

She didn't say she would never *come back,* I reminded myself. *She just said it wouldn't be tomorrow like she'd originally planned.*

Well, I'd tell him when he came back inside. I wasn't about to ruin his time out in the sun and the wind with some very unexpected—and unpleasant—news.

No, I sat there on the couch and forced myself to drink the rest of my tea, and eventually the two familiars came back inside, looking windblown and content.

That probably wouldn't last for very long...not in Lionel's case, anyway.

I forced a smile as the hedgehog trundled into the room and sat down on the rug by the hearth. Milo followed and lay down a few feet away, tongue lolling in a doggy smile.

"Hey," I said, and prayed I sounded mostly natural. "I just heard from Sela."

At once, Milo's floppy ears pricked up, and Lionel tilted his head.

"She's coming to get me tomorrow, right?"

"Well, not exactly," I replied, trying not to wince when I saw the hedgehog almost visibly deflate. "She's running a little late, but she said she'd be here sometime next week. She just isn't sure when. So, that means you get to hang out with Milo and me for just a little bit longer. Doesn't that sound like fun?"

Lionel glanced over at Milo and back at me. "Oh, sure," he said, his squeaky voice flatter than usual. "That'll be fine."

At once, Milo got up and went over to the hedgehog, and gave his tiny ear a solemn lick. "I'm sorry your mistress isn't coming home when she said she would," he told Lionel. "But Charity and I will take good care of you until she comes back." A pause, and the cocker spaniel gave me a solemn look. "And we'll have Noah come over tonight so we can all have takeout together, right?"

How could I turn down those big brown puppy-dog eyes? I would have much rather preferred to fly solo tonight in the hope that my bruise might settle a bit before the next time I saw Noah Jenkins, but it didn't look as though such a delay was in the cards.

No, right now the important thing was to keep Lionel as happy as possible.

"Sure," I said stoutly. "I'll text him right away."

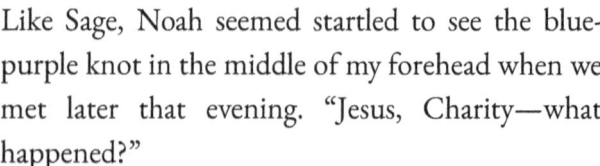

Like Sage, Noah seemed startled to see the blue-purple knot in the middle of my forehead when we met later that evening. "Jesus, Charity—what happened?"

"I fell," I said blithely. "I was an idiot and went exploring where I shouldn't. But I'm fine—really."

"Exploring where?"

Because I hadn't found a single witchy thing down in the tunnels, I didn't even hesitate before replying, "Oh, turns out the shop cellar is connected to the old smugglers' tunnels under Salem. But I didn't get too far before I tripped over a rock and went flying. Honestly, there isn't much to see down there."

"I didn't even know there were tunnels," he said as he followed me into the kitchen.

Clearly, even though Noah had been living here for more than a year, he hadn't yet picked up on all the local area knowledge.

"There are," I replied, then opened the refrigerator door. "White, or rosé?"

For a second, he didn't say anything. Then, quietly, "Are you sure you should be drinking after smacking yourself on the head like that?"

I waved a careless hand and smiled blithely. "Oh, it's no big deal. No dizziness, no headaches. I'm sure I didn't get even a little bitty concussion."

All right, that was a very small lie about the headache and the dizziness. But because both symptoms had gone away quickly enough, I had to believe that my tumble hadn't caused any lasting issues.

Again, Noah didn't reply right away. Then his shoulders lifted, and I got the feeling he was telling himself I was a big girl and could take care of myself.

"Rosé, then...we're getting Thai, right?"

"That was the plan," I said, and reached for the bottle of rosé. Noah went ahead and got down a couple of glasses from the cupboard, and I gave a nod to his concern for my health by pouring myself a smaller amount than I normally would have.

The weather had remained gorgeous, so we both went outside with our glasses of wine and took a seat at the table and chairs on the patio. Milo and Lionel were already out in the garden, and Noah's serious expression lightened as he caught sight of the two familiars lying on the grass under the oak tree.

"Lionel looks like he's doing well."

"He is," I agreed. "And you'll never guess—I heard from Sela earlier today."

If I'd just told Noah that aliens had landed on my lawn that morning and given me the secret for world peace, he couldn't have looked any more shocked.

"You did?" he said. "What did she say?"

"That she's planning to be back sometime next week, but not tomorrow the way she'd originally planned," I replied. "I couldn't get anything more out of her except that."

"Did you ask about Anna?" Noah asked then, eyes narrowing.

"In a roundabout kind of way," I said. "Sela made it sound as if she already knew."

His forehead creased in a frown, although I couldn't be sure whether he was simply downright mystified or actually angry that Sela was acting so cavalier about her sister's death. "And she still isn't coming back?"

"Not immediately." I paused to sip some rosé and added, "It all sounds pretty awful, I know. I just can't figure out what's going on with her. It almost feels as if she's waiting for something to happen before she returns, but I have absolutely no idea what it might be."

Like me, Noah seemed to decide the best thing to do right now was have a swallow of wine. After-ward, though, he remarked, "This whole situation is getting crazier and crazier."

"I know," I said. "The only good thing is that at least now I've heard from Sela, even if I can't begin to explain her behavior."

"That makes two of us." Noah went silent for a moment, expression still perplexed. "I just can't imagine anyone staying away when they knew they'd lost a sibling. If anything ever happened to one of my sisters, I'd be on the first plane home, no matter what."

I made a sympathetic noise. Not having any brothers or sisters of my own, I couldn't exactly imagine what such a bond might feel like. Despite that lack, I had to believe I would do the same thing under similar circumstances, especially since I could easily imagine how it would feel if one of my fellow coven members died unexpectedly. It wasn't quite the same thing as losing family, but still, all those women had been a part of my life for as long as I could remember. I didn't want to think what it would be like to suddenly have them gone.

"Well, Sela must have her reasons," I said. "Even if none of us can figure out what they might be. I guess all we can do now is wait for her to get back."

"And explain herself," Noah remarked, his tone now grim. "I'm sure we'd all like to hear what she was thinking."

That was for sure. Now, though, all we could do was wait...and hope Sela wouldn't extend her trip past this next week.

And if that happened, well, I supposed I'd figure it out when the time came.

Chapter 14

Dangling Threads

THAT SUNDAY FELT...WEIRD. I'D BEEN thinking for so long that Sela would be back today to pick up Lionel, and even though I knew she wouldn't be coming, wasn't exactly sure when she'd finally arrive in Salem to retrieve her familiar, I couldn't quite keep my thoughts from going to all the things it would require to get him packed up and ready to go.

Not that there was much to do. I'd had to get him a fresh bag of cat food, because what Sela had supplied wouldn't have lasted even a week, let alone ten-plus days. And he'd grown so attached to his basket that I knew I would have to send it along with him, although that might actually make him easier to transport.

Both Lionel and Milo didn't seem too upset by

the change in plans, so I did my best to roll with it. At the same time, though, I couldn't shake this odd sensation of dissonance, as if there was something else lurking in the back of my mind, something I'd forgotten but was of vital importance.

But I'd learned a long time ago that trying to force it would only make matters worse, so I did my best to focus on my usual Sunday activities—doing laundry, cleaning the kitchen and bathrooms, dusting and vacuuming. Noah hadn't stayed late the night before, telling me he'd promised to go down to Boston to help his brother-in-law and his youngest sister clean out their garage.

I'd joked that I hoped they were paying him well in beer, and he'd admitted one of the reasons he'd agreed to give up his Sunday was to get some of his brother-in-law's smoked brisket.

"Well, and they're also expecting their second kid," Noah had explained, "and Matt really wants to get the garage cleared out so they can park at least one car in there. Beth said she wasn't dragging a stroller through the snow for one more winter."

It seemed like a good reason to me for taking on such a project, and even though I knew I would miss Noah, I wasn't about to ask him to cancel his plans and stay with me just because I was feeling hinky. The two familiars would be company enough to keep me from feeling too alone.

After I was done with my chores, though, I went and got my laptop and set it on the kitchen table, figuring I could do a little research on the tunnels, see if there was any point in my going back down there...even though I'd already vowed to myself that I never wanted to set foot in those dim passageways again.

A lot of what I wanted to find was hidden behind paywalls, but it definitely looked to me as though I'd been exploring a section that hadn't been mapped very well. In fact, the two diagrams I was able to locate made it seem as if the smugglers' tunnels only extended about a block past Salem Commons, which wasn't nearly close enough to get to my cellar on Essex Street.

Well, what I'd been able to locate had been compiled by local history buffs, not professional historians, so I supposed there was always the chance that they hadn't done enough exploring, or were basing their blog posts on word-of-mouth that wasn't very accurate. I'd definitely done the correct thing by heading southeast, because if I'd gone the other way, I would have ended up in charted territory and not found anything of much interest.

Not that I'd found much the way I'd gone, either. After I'd regained consciousness, I'd shone the flashlight down the passageway ahead of me, just to make sure I wasn't missing something important, but all I'd seen was more tunnel, and maybe a dark blur at the end of my range of vision that could have been a wall or a curve in the passage.

It definitely hadn't been anything significant enough to make me want to go back down there. And, as far as I could tell, if the smugglers had left anything valuable behind, it had been scooped up decades before I came along.

So, that seemed to settle that. I had no doubt Noah would be relieved I'd back-burnered any further expeditions to Salem's tunnels, but if anything, the bit of research I'd just done made me feel even more restless.

On a whim, I picked up my phone and touched the button to send a call to Grace Bowersby.

When she answered, she sounded a little startled. Most of the time, I didn't just call her out of the blue. "Charity?"

"Hi, Grace," I replied. "I was wondering if you could tell me something about the tunnels under the town. Do you have any record of any witches ever using them?"

"Not that I'm aware of," she said, her tone still somewhat surprised, as if she couldn't quite figure out why I'd gone off on this particular tangent.

"They were built a long time after the witch trials —in the mid-1700s, if I'm not mistaken. But I'll admit that I haven't done any in-depth studies on them, mostly because they really don't have any connection to witch history."

Hmm. I'd really been hoping that Grace might have some helpful tidbits to offer, something I couldn't find in any of the blogs and other online resources I'd been able to access.

"I went on one of the tours once," she added, surprising me. "Just to see what the tunnels were like. But even though the tour guide had some interesting details to offer that I hadn't heard of before, there wasn't anything he said that would connect the tunnels to us witches. Good thing, too, or otherwise, we might have had to do something about it."

What that "something" might have been, I didn't know. A gentle spell to convince the tour company that those particular details didn't need to be passed along to the general public, or something a little stronger, an enchantment to make everyone involved forget that they'd ever existed at all?

As soon as that thought went through my head, I experienced an odd little twinge, as though the notion of making the tour guides forget anything regarding witches and tunnels had more significance than I would have given it credit for. But because I couldn't really figure out why it might be especially important, I dismissed it from my mind.

"Well, thanks," I said. "I just thought I'd ask."

"Any particular reason?"

We coven members generally didn't keep secrets from one another, and that was why I went ahead and told Grace the story about the rat running over my foot, the crashed shelving unit, and the passageway that had been revealed through the broken wall.

"I didn't find anything interesting," I said. "So, tomorrow I'm going to call my contractor and have him come out to give me a bid on repairing the wall."

"Probably a good thing," Grace replied. "All sorts of nasty things could come through there. Still, it's interesting that the tunnel extends so far. The tour guide told us the tunnels were situated mainly near Salem Commons."

Exactly the same thing I'd already known. "Well, considering I tripped and fell and gave myself a nice bump on the head, the people who do those tours probably decided it was too dangerous to let anyone go past the section they've already explored."

Grace made a concerned sound. "Are you all right?"

"I'm fine," I assured her. I knew I needed to downplay my accident as much as I could, because otherwise, she'd go telling tales to my mother, and then I'd never hear the end of it. "But I can see why people stay out of those other parts of the tunnel system. For all I know, it's blocked off on the west side. I didn't go that way, so I can't say for sure."

"Definitely best to stay out," she agreed. "But now I need to go—I need to get my lemon bars out of the oven."

Since Grace's lemon bars were legendary, I didn't want to do anything that might make her over-bake them. I said a hasty goodbye and ended the call. As I set my phone down on the coffee table, though, I had another one of those odd sensations, as though I was missing something crucial but couldn't get my recalcitrant brain to identify exactly what it was.

Maybe I really had gotten a mild concussion.

If that was the case, I probably should have been resting today rather than running around the house, doing my best to get everything tidied up and ready for a new week. But I didn't feel particularly fatigued and wasn't dizzy at all, so maybe I was worrying about nothing.

I got up from the couch and headed into the kitchen. Maybe it was time to see if I had enough of the necessary ingredients to throw something interesting into the crockpot.

By the time Monday morning rolled around, I was all too glad to head into work. I didn't really like knowing I still had that gaping hole in my basement wall, but I hoped I'd be able to get Stu Abernathy out here sooner rather than later to get it patched up.

In fact, because I got to the store a little early, I went ahead and made the call. Since Stu never seemed to get rattled by anything, he didn't sound surprised by the report that I'd managed to punch through the wall in the cellar, but only told me he could be there in the next half hour.

Perfect. That would still be after we opened, but the Monday morning hours I'd added to the shop schedule hadn't turned out to be busy so far —to the point that I knew I wouldn't extend the experiment past the Fourth of July holiday—and I knew Sage could handle things while I was down in the basement with the contractor.

"Feeling better?" she asked.

"Much," I said. "Thanks for covering for me on Saturday."

"No worries." Her gaze went to my forehead, but by that point, the bump had pretty much receded, and any lingering discoloration had been easy to cover up with some concealer and foundation. "It was busy, but I wasn't swamped."

Exactly what I'd wanted to hear. She hadn't said much when she dropped off the key late on Saturday afternoon, but that was because she'd been on her way to meet some friends for yet another outing, this one up in Lowell somewhere.

Well, it was nice that one of us had a social life.

I kicked that foolish thought to the curb just as soon as it popped up. Maybe I wasn't running all over the place like Sage, but I had a steady thing going with Noah, and his friends seemed to have accepted me just fine. We went out to dinner together, went sailing in Jared's boat when favorable weather happened to line up with one of my days off. I had absolutely nothing to complain about, especially when I contrasted my life as it was now with the way it had been even a month ago.

After letting Sage know that Stu would be here soon to look at the basement, I went ahead and unlocked the front door. No one was waiting outside, but I didn't mind. It was always kind of nice to start the week off slowly instead of getting hit in the face with mobs of shoppers right off the bat.

Several people did trickle into the store, but they were regulars, the kind of patrons who bought the same thing month after month, so it was easy enough to take care of their orders.

And then Stu came in. Obviously, he wasn't a part of the witch community, but he'd done work for my mother since before I was even born, and for Sage's family as well.

She called out a greeting, and he nodded in reply. Like a lot of New Englanders, he was a man of few words. I still didn't know his exact age, but I guessed he had to be at least in his late sixties, maybe even his early seventies. He was of medium height, wiry, with the kind of features that didn't seem to age, more like got burnished over time, the tanned skin stretched taut across his high cheek-bones, his hazel eyes keen beneath their hooded lids.

"The basement?" he said to me in lieu of hello.

"This way," I replied.

I led him down the steep wooden stairs and into the cellar. Because I'd been anticipating his visit, I'd already come down here to turn on the lights. The fluorescent fixtures clearly illuminated the large hole in the wall and the mess of bricks and powdery mortar on the floor.

"Ah," was his only comment...not that I'd expected much more than that.

He went over to the wall and looked at the jagged edges of the hole, then picked up a couple of the bricks and hefted them in his hand. What that was supposed to tell him, I had no idea, but he was the contractor, not me.

After setting the bricks down, he fished a

penlight out of one of the pockets of his faded Levi's before going around to the exterior of the hole, shining his flashlight on the other side of the wall.

I knew better than to ask what he was seeing. When he was ready to tell me, he would.

Instead, I waited there in what I hoped didn't feel like impatient silence, hands planted on the hips of my black sleeveless dress. A moment or two passed, and then Stu stepped back inside the cellar.

"I can fix it," he said, which didn't surprise me very much. So far, I hadn't come across an issue he couldn't handle, although I suppose he might have balked at being asked to construct an entire house.

Or maybe not. I knew he'd built Grace Bowersby's garage for her when the old one—constructed sometime in the 1930s—had decided to collapse after a particularly heavy snowfall one January.

Asking how much the repairs were going to cost would be gauche, so I only nodded. Stu was honest and never overcharged his clients, so I didn't have to worry about that. It would cost what it cost, and not a penny more or less.

"When can you get started?"

"Tomorrow," he replied. "I thought maybe I'd have to source bricks to match, but it's pretty obvious this hole was closed up recently. This stuff is kinda new."

And he pointed at the clutter of broken bricks on the floor near his feet.

Surprised, I looked down at the bricks and then back up at him. "Really? It's not as old as the rest of the tunnel?"

One corner of his mouth lifted, which was about the closest he would ever let himself get to a smile. "Nah. Tunnel's stone, mostly, except for some old patches. Looks like these bricks were put in here no more than ten years ago. That's my best guess, anyway."

So...the hole had existed for a while, but a decade ago—maybe even sooner than that—someone had decided to close it up.

Why?

Well, having a ginormous hole in your basement isn't a very good look, I thought.

But the point was, the hole had been open before that, and then for whatever reason, it had been sealed off and the wall plastered over to make it look as if it had never been there at all.

Weird.

I'd bought the store a little more than five years ago, proud of my ability to pay for it myself. True, I'd been saving up, peddling my elixirs and tinctures at various fairs and swap meets and farmers' markets, but still, it had been a stretch, one I might not have been able to manage if my mother hadn't kicked in the final few thousand dollars for me to make the down payment. Afterward, the business had done well enough that her loan to me was already paid off.

A thought tickled my mind, one I couldn't quite ignore.

What if someone had sealed up the basement once they knew I was buying the store?

On the surface, that didn't seem so odd. Obviously, the previous owner—Emerson Gates, the rare instrument dealer—had wanted to make sure the property was in the best shape possible so it would fetch a good price.

But why would Emerson have kept a big old hole in his basement in the first place?

Maybe he didn't even know it was there, I thought next. *After all, the cellar is damp and musty on a good day, not the kind of place anyone would want to store a Stradivarius.*

The next question was, even if Emerson didn't know the hole was there, someone must have. The same person who'd sealed it up once they knew the property was being sold, not wanting to take the risk that the next owner wouldn't be quite as averse to using the basement as Mr. Gates.

If I'd uttered those suspicions aloud, I probably would have sounded like someone who hung out too much on conspiracy theory forums. But after everything that had happened lately—not just Anna Warren's suspicious death, but the deaths of Trevor Miller and Darla Fitzgerald as well—I was inclined to believe there was a whole hell of a lot going on under the surface than I could ever have imagined.

"So, you want me to go ahead and get the materials?" Stu prompted, probably because I'd been standing there in silence rather than responding to his comment about when he'd thought the hole had been filled.

"Um, yes, yes," I replied quickly. "That would be great. You can do the work whenever it's convenient—it's not like we have to worry about bugging my customers with the construction."

He didn't smile, only gave me a slight tilt of his head. "Yeah, let me go to the builders' yard and see what I can get. Should be able to get started late morning tomorrow, probably. Good thing you caught me now—I've got a project for a new stone wall I'm starting on Wednesday."

Good thing, for sure. Even with modern equipment, constructing a stone wall was involved, back-breaking work, something that would most likely keep him occupied for at least the next couple of weeks.

"It's definitely a good thing," I agreed. "Thanks again for coming on such short notice."

He inclined his head again, then headed for the stairs. I followed, my thoughts racing.

Someone had plugged that hole in the basement wall before I could take ownership of the store.

I needed to find out why.

Chapter 15

Forgotten Melody

As usually happened when I needed to know something quickly—even though this time it wasn't strictly witch-related—I called Grace Bowersby.

"What can you tell me about Emerson Gates?" I asked as soon as she picked up her phone.

"Isn't he the man who owned your shop before you bought it?"

"Yes."

A flummoxed silence followed my answer. Then she said, "I really don't know much about him. He collected vintage instruments, and I believe he was once a concert cellist. But at some point, he decided to stop touring and come home to Salem. That had to be at least twenty years ago, though, probably more."

This wasn't much more than I already knew, and I found myself frowning. "You don't know anything else about him? Nothing at all?"

A sigh came through my iPhone's speaker, a brief gust of breath that sounded partly amused, partly exasperated. "Why would I know anything? He had nothing to do with the witch community, so the only reason I knew he existed at all was because I would walk past his shop when I was taking a stroll on Essex Street."

I probably should have expected an answer like that. When I'd opened negotiations with Emerson's real estate agent, it was clear neither one of them had any idea who I was, other than a prospective buyer for his property. And that was how it should be. We witches went out of our way to make sure the mundies had no idea who we were, and since it was obvious that Emerson hadn't been married to a witch, there was no way he could have known I was a magical practitioner.

Honestly, I didn't even know why I kept thinking the hole in my basement had anything to do with the magical community. I'd gone exploring down there and hadn't found a damn thing. It was only that annoying tickle at the back of my mind, the one which seemed to be trying to tell me there was more here than met the eye.

"Well, I just thought I should ask," I told Grace. "But thanks for letting me know."

"Of course," she replied. "You take care, Charity. We're concerned about you."

She ended the call there, although her parting words seemed to indicate she thought I wasn't taking it easy enough, and must have mentioned my spill to other members of the coven.

Honestly, I was kind of surprised my mother hadn't called to check up on me, although I guessed she knew I would have only reiterated that I was fine and that I didn't need her hovering.

All right, I probably wouldn't have been quite that rude, but the impression would have been accurate.

The morning ticked along, and then, a little before noon, Derek Falco came into the shop.

My first instinct was to put my hand up to my forehead to hide the bruise there, although I managed to refrain. Not that it was any business of his whether I went exploring in the tunnels under Salem...or maybe it was, if that kind of expedition involved trespassing...but still, I didn't feel like having to explain away the discolored mark on my face.

However, either my makeup skills were better than I thought or he wasn't paying close attention, because he said, "I heard you took a little trip over to Marblehead."

"So?" I responded. "I wasn't aware that was illegal."

"It's not," Derek said with one of his velvety smiles. It didn't seem to have quite the same effect on me I'd expected it to, probably because I was smart enough to realize that, no matter how good-looking Detective Falco might be, he still wasn't Noah Jenkins. "But it still annoyed Chuck Finley."

"He knew I went to see Barri Novak?" I asked, genuinely surprised. Not that I'd been trying to hide the visit or anything, but still, I didn't recall seeing Detective Finley anywhere near Barri's pub.

"Apparently," Derek replied. "He saw you coming out of the Driftwood Tavern just as he was driving up. Sounds like he wanted to ask Barri Novak a few additional questions."

I shrugged, then paused so I could glance over at Sage. She was currently explaining the dosage for my insomnia elixir to an older man whose bright Hawaiian shirt and Birkenstocks seemed to proclaim he wasn't from around here, but I still got the impression that she was attempting to listen to my conversation with Derek Falco as best she could.

My shoulders went up in what I hoped was a halfway believable shrug. "I figured that Colin's family was the best chance I had for trying to figure out where Sela might have gone." I paused, then asked, "Did you know that Colin had been in contact with his family?"

"I did," Derek responded. "Chuck told me. But it still seems like he was being pretty cagey about where he and Sela actually were."

"Barri Novak told me the same thing," I said, which felt safe enough.

Should I tell him that Sela had texted me yesterday?

Almost as soon as that thought popped up in my mind, I shot it down. Technically, the Marblehead police—let alone the Salem P.D.—weren't even investigating Sela Warren, so there was no reason for me to divulge that piece of information. Besides, she hadn't told me anything that was of much use, couldn't even pin down the exact day she thought she'd be back in Salem, so there wasn't much point in passing on such a fiddly data point.

"Really, I didn't hear anything from Barri that was very helpful," I went on. "Only that Colin's family really seems to like Sela, so I don't have any reason to believe any of them would want her—or her sister—to come to any harm."

"But Anna died of a brain aneurysm," Derek said, eyes narrowing slightly.

Oops. I couldn't even blame my slip-up on a concussion, since I was pretty sure that physically I was fine.

"Right, I know," I said hastily. "I just mean that Colin's family seems lovely, and I'm glad Sela will have them there to help her out when she comes back and finds out...."

I let the words trail off there, mostly because I didn't see the point in continuing. Derek knew exactly what I was talking about.

"They do seem to be nice people," he commented, tone so neutral that I guessed he was still trying to figure out what I'd really meant by my blunder of a comment, even if he wasn't going to press me on the subject.

"I was just trying to fill in some of the blanks," I said next. "That's all. But other than hearing Colin had texted his mom, I didn't learn anything." I stopped there, figuring I'd said enough.

Derek didn't reply at once, and a sharp thrill of alarm went through me.

Was he going to ask me why I hadn't told Barri Novak where her son and his new wife really were?

But instead he inquired, "Wasn't Sela supposed to be back yesterday?"

Well, the man could do math, that was for sure. "Yes," I said, praying I looked like a woman worried she was going to be stuck with a hedgehog forever, and not someone who at least knew the animal's mistress planned to be back sometime this week. "Good thing hedgehogs don't have much of a time sense."

Derek's mouth quirked in response to my comment, as I'd hoped it would, but then his expression turned serious as he asked, "Is it going to be hard for you to keep watching him?"

"Lionel?" I asked, then went on without waiting for a reply, "No, not at all. He's such a tiny thing—he doesn't eat much, and he's gotten pretty attached to my dog. I know I can trust Milo to keep an eye on him while I'm at work. I'm more worried about what's going on with Sela."

"I guess all we can do is hope she'll be in touch soon," Derek said. "And if you need any help with him, I'm sure someone at the humane society would be willing to pitch in."

Even though I knew the workers at our local shelter were amazing people, there was no way in the world I'd ever send Lionel to a shelter, not while he had a safe home with me and Milo, and not when so many other lost and neglected creatures needed to take refuge there.

"It's fine," I assured him. "This kind of thing happens sometimes when you foster animals."

Technically, I wasn't fostering Lionel, just pet-sitting him, but Derek didn't question my choice of words. "It's good to know he's safe with you."

It looked as though he wanted to say something else, but right then, Sage wrapped up her sale with the tourist in the loud shirt, and Detective Falco apparently decided it was better to leave things there for now.

"Anyway, just wanted to check in," he said, in a

slightly louder voice. Then he tipped his head toward Sage and went outside, following a few feet behind the Hawaiian shirt–bedecked customer.

"What was that about?" Sage inquired, her expression a little too curious.

"Nothing," I said. "He was just following up on a couple of things about Sela. But I didn't have anything new to tell him."

Luckily, my assistant couldn't call out that lie to my face, since I hadn't said anything to Sage, either, about those texts from Sela on Saturday afternoon. Like everyone else in our coven, she believed the Marblehead witch was completely MIA.

"Ah, got it," she said, then seemed to guess from my expression that I didn't want to share any more words on the subject of Derek Falco, because she headed over to one of the displays and began straightening the bottles.

It was busywork, but I wouldn't keep her from it. At least that way, there was less chance of her asking questions I had no intention of answering.

Noah came over with takeout again that night. I'd offered for us to go to his place, but he only told me he thought it would better for us to stay at my house for dinner. Although he didn't come out and say it, I knew he was concerned about Lionel as well now that Sela was late in showing up. True, an ordinary hedgehog probably wouldn't have been able to tell his mistress had missed her deadline, but I knew this was Noah's empathy showing itself again, and I hadn't bothered to argue with him.

So many reasons why I knew I was falling hard for that man.

We had pizza and offered Milo morsels of pepperoni and Lionel little bites of olive, a treat he'd obviously never had before.

"These are so good!" he exclaimed, although to Noah, I knew the hedgehog's words would have only sounded like squeaks of joy.

"Who knew hedgehogs were such fiends for olives?" he remarked after offering another tiny bit of black olive to the familiar, who snatched it up and downed it with gusto.

"Not me," I said with a grin. It really did feel good to sit there in my comfortably shabby dining room and drink a red blend from California and not think of much of anything except the two familiars and how much fun they were having getting their own little tastes of the pizza Noah and I were sharing. "But this is just another reason why I don't mind that Sela is late to pick him up."

Noah had been smiling as well, but the expression faded a little as he looked down at Lionel. "What happens if she doesn't come?"

Although I knew that wasn't going to happen...probably...I answered his question seriously. "Then he'll stay with me and Milo. He's such a little bitty thing—it's not like I'd be adopting someone's Great Dane or anything close to it."

Noah's hand went to touch mine where it lay on the tabletop. Such a small caress, and yet it still seemed to carry a wealth of meaning. "Why did I know that was exactly what you'd say?"

I didn't reply, only looked back at him. In unspoken agreement, we set our napkins aside, then headed for the stairs.

The rest of the pizza would have to wait.

Later—after we'd cleared away the remnants of dinner, and I'd waved goodbye to Noah as he drove off in his Toyota Tundra—I lay in the bed we'd shared a short time earlier and stared at the ceiling. I wanted to believe Sela would come back for Lionel, but if she didn't, that was okay, too. The little guy was adorable and wouldn't be much trouble at all.

No, far more pressing was the conundrum of

the hole in my basement wall. Stu would be at the shop to fix it tomorrow, so the physical reminder of its presence would be gone soon enough, and yet my mind kept picking at the problem, wondering why anyone would have left it open all those years, only to finally plug it when it came time to sell the property.

As far as I knew, Emerson Gates was still living in Salem. Retired, of course, but I hadn't heard from anyone that he'd left town, and that was the kind of casual gossip someone probably would have passed along to me, simply because I now owned the shop that had been his for so many years.

Would there be any point in going to talk to him?

I didn't know. There was a perfectly innocent reason why the wall in the basement would have been fixed a few years ago—namely, that the defect wouldn't exactly improve the store's property value —but my gut kept telling me it was more than that.

If I could even find out where he lived.

Well, that part was easy enough.

I reached for my phone where it sat on my nightstand, entered "Emerson Gates, Salem, Massachusetts" in my browser's search engine, and took a look at the results.

Yes, right there on Warren Street. Clearly, he

hadn't bothered to do anything to hide his current whereabouts.

So, sometime tomorrow...after Stu had showed up to fix the basement wall and things at the store felt quiet enough for me to slip out...I'd go have a few words with Emerson.

Whether he'd have anything of use to tell me was debatable, but for now, it was the only lead I had to go on.

Stu Abernathy was not the sort of person to wait until the store opened at ten so he could start working. No, he was right there at eight o'clock, and wore the expression of someone who would have preferred to begin work even earlier.

"I'll be right upstairs," I told him after he set down his tools and informed me he'd be going back and forth from his truck so he could bring the bricks down to the basement. "Just let me know if you need anything."

He made a "hmph" sound that seemed to indicate he wouldn't reach out unless he had a heart attack...and maybe not even then. His response appeared to be my signal that I needed to stay out of the way and let him do his work, which was what I intended to do.

But puttering around the shop only took so much time, and I gave an annoyed glance at the clock on one wall. Nine twenty-two, which felt way too early to go knocking on Emerson Gates's door. No, I'd have to wait until Sage showed up, and then I could see about paying him a visit.

To my utter relief, she appeared about ten minutes early, possibly trying to make up for being late the day before. She'd barely had time to tuck her purse into the cubbyhole under the front counter before I said, "Can you watch the store for about a half hour or so? Stu's working in the basement, and I have an errand I need to run."

An inquiring light showed in her hazel eyes, but she didn't ask any questions, only said, "Sure. It should be pretty quiet until closer to lunch."

I thanked her, grabbed my purse, and went out back to get into my SUV. With Stu occupying the third spot behind the shop, there was always a chance I wouldn't be able to get my preferred parking space when I returned, but I was willing to take that chance. This might turn out to be nothing more than a wild goose chase, and yet I needed to hear what Emerson had to say about the hole in my basement wall.

His house was about five minutes away from the store, only a few blocks over from Noah's rented house. Emerson's home looked like it also dated to the late 1800s or maybe the turn of the century, an imposing two-story structure whose inspiration seemed more Craftsman than farmhouse, with its wide porch and multi-paned windows, and seemed like exactly the kind of place you might find a retired concert cellist.

I got out of my SUV and made my way up the front walk, all the while praying Emerson wasn't a night owl who didn't rise until one or two in the afternoon. If that turned out to be the case, he'd be cranky before we even got started.

However, he answered the door promptly enough in response to my knock, and was fully dressed, in a white button-down shirt and dark blue cardigan that seemed way too warm for the late-June day.

Since I wasn't here to comment on his sartorial choices, I only smiled and said, "Good morning, Mr. Gates. My name is Charity Hughes. I was hoping I could talk to you for a moment."

His keen gray eyes narrowed just the slightest bit, as if trying to place the name. The sale of the store had been handled entirely by his real estate agent, so we'd never actually met in person. "You're the girl who bought my store, aren't you?"

"Yes," I replied. "Do you have time to talk?"

No hesitation, nothing that would make me believe he was questioning my motives for showing up on his doorstep out of the blue. Then again, why would he have any reason to think this was anything more than a friendly chat?

"Of course," he said graciously. "Come inside."

He held the door open a little wider, and I entered a large room beautifully appointed with all the original dark wood trim, the built-ins on either side of the stone fireplace filled with a tasteful collection of *objets d'art* that I guessed he must have gathered when he was traveling the world as a concert cellist.

"Would you like some water?" he asked. "I just put together a pitcher with some lemon slices from my garden."

That sounded wonderful; now that I was here, my throat was a little dry. Nerves, I guessed. "Yes, please."

"Have a seat. I'll be right back."

I went and sat down on the caramel leather sofa, doing my best to look as though I didn't have any ulterior motives for being here. A moment later, Emerson returned, a glass of ice water with a lush lemon slice floating in it in each of his hands.

After handing me one of the glasses, he sat down in the wood-framed chair to the right of the couch. "Now, what can I do for you, Ms. Hughes?"

"Charity," I said with a smile. "Actually, it's about that hole in the basement wall at the shop."

While he didn't exactly stiffen, something

about the set of his shoulders appeared a little more tense than it had a moment earlier. However, his tone was genial enough as he replied, "Is it giving you trouble? I doubt that the crew who did the work would offer any kind of warranty since the wall was repaired so long ago, but—"

"No, that's all right," I cut in. The last thing I wanted him to think was that I was here to extort money from him to have the wall fixed again. "I'm taking care of it, since it was my own clumsiness that opened up the hole this time. But I'm kind of curious about why it was there in the first place."

"To connect to the smugglers' tunnels, of course," Emerson said. "I thought it was an interesting piece of local history, and that was why I didn't bother to have it closed until I decided to sell the place. I never used the basement, anyway—too damp down there to make it at all suitable for storing my inventory."

Which was about what I'd thought. And while I supposed his reason for not sealing the hole sounded valid enough, something about it still didn't ring true.

"And that's the only reason why you left it open all those years?"

Now he looked almost guilty. "Well...I suppose Tonya might have helped convince me it wasn't worth repairing."

"'Tonya'?" I repeated, not sure I'd heard him right. "Tonya Willis?"

"Oh, you know her?" Emerson asked, his expression showing nothing more than simple curiosity.

"She's a friend of my mother's," I lied. After all, I couldn't exactly admit that we were in the same coven. Knowing her through my mother seemed plausible enough, since they were only about five years apart in age. "How do you know her?"

"We were...acquainted...once upon a time," he said. "But we don't see each other much now."

That sounded like a roundabout way of confessing that they'd once been intimate. I didn't know why I should be so surprised, except Emerson must have had at least a decade on Tonya.

Then again, he was still tall and slim and handsome in a fine-hewn sort of way, like an elegant tree that had grown only more graceful as the years wore on. I supposed I could see why Tonya Willis might have been attracted to him, and that was without throwing the whole world-renowned cellist thing into the mix.

As soon as that thought passed through my mind, I wanted to smack myself on the forehead. How could I not have seen it?

Tonya's daughter, Aria, was a gifted violinist who played for the Vermont Symphony Orchestra and taught violin and piano on the side. That was why she'd moved to Burlington about a year and a half ago—she'd been invited to play with the orchestra, a real honor for someone who'd just turned twenty-five.

No wonder she was so talented...and no wonder why Tonya had given her daughter a musical name. It was a little tip of the hat to the man who'd obviously passed on those musical genes.

"Aria's your daughter," I said quietly.

He gave a rueful little chuckle. "I see you've figured it out. Tonya never wanted me to acknowledge Aria publicly, and at first, I was all right with that. But then I realized I was going to miss out on seeing my daughter grow up, so I stopped touring and came back to Salem, bought the store. I wasn't as much a part of Aria's life as I would have liked, but at least I was here, could listen to her play at school concerts, that kind of thing. It was better than not getting to see her at all."

I nodded, knowing there wasn't much else I could say. This sort of thing was fairly common in the witch community, since most of us wanted children but weren't lucky enough to find someone we could trust with the knowledge of who we were. Some, like my mother, opted for artificial insemination, but many others simply chose someone they thought had good genetic material to pass along.

In Emerson's case, it was abundantly clear why Tonya Willis had selected him.

"So...." It really wasn't my place to comment on his relationship with Aria, so instead I said, "Tonya didn't think you needed to close up the hole in the basement?"

"No," Emerson replied. "She said it was kind of fun, even convinced me to explore the tunnels with her a little. And then as the years went on and the two of us drifted apart, I sort of forgot about the tunnels and the hole in the basement wall, since I never went down there. It wasn't until I was getting the shop ready for sale that I realized I really had to do something about it. That was when I hired a crew to come in and brick it up." He stopped there, now looking almost apologetic. "It appears they didn't do a very good job, or it wouldn't have fallen down just because you had an 'accident.'"

"Oh, I did a pretty good job of it," I assured him. "I managed to knock a whole shelving unit into the wall after a rat ran across my foot. So you really don't need to worry about that."

"Ah, that's what happened?" He shook his head, but now his gray eyes twinkled a bit, rather than appearing worried. "Still, I'd be happy to help with the repairs."

"No, really, it's okay," I said. "It just felt like kind of a mystery, but now you've cleared it up."

"Part of it, anyway," Emerson commented. "I

tried to do some research to find out if the shop had once been owned by anyone connected to the smugglers who built the tunnels in the center of town, but I wasn't able to discover very much. Records in those days weren't what they are now, and anyone involved in smuggling would have worked hard to hide their activities."

I couldn't really argue with that observation, so I only nodded. After taking a sip of my lemon water, I set the glass down on one of the coasters that rested on the coffee table and rose to my feet. "Well, thank you for taking some time out of your day to let me know about the basement," I said. "I really need to get back to my shop, though—I don't want to leave my assistant handling things there for too long."

"It was a pleasure to talk to you," he said. "I don't get too many visitors these days."

What in the world was I supposed to say in reply to that comment? I think I managed an awkward little smile, then took a few steps toward the door. I paused there, though, my hand on the knob, and ventured, "Does Aria know?"

He gave a sorrowful shake of his head. "Tonya didn't want me to tell her, and I respected her wishes. A very independent woman, Tonya Willis."

As were most witches.

We had to be.

Still, I found myself saying, "You should tell

your daughter," before I slipped out onto the porch. Maybe that was stepping way outside my bounds, but he'd looked so sad.

No matter what Tonya might think on the subject, Aria Willis deserved to know the truth about her father.

Chapter 16

What Dreams May Come

I WAS FEELING MELANCHOLY AS I DROVE back to the store, although I did my best to tell myself none of this was my business. Maybe Emerson would find the courage to tell his daughter he was her absent father and maybe he wouldn't, but in the meantime, I still had Anna Warren's mysterious death to worry about, as well as whether Sela would actually show up sometime this week the way she'd promised.

And that didn't even take into account the hole in the basement wall. True, Emerson had explained away most of the mystery, even if I still couldn't quite understand why Tonya would have advised him to keep it open. But everyone had their own whims and whimsies, although Tonya tended to be a very no-nonsense kind of witch. I supposed she had to be, considering her work required her to

handle high-end real estate transactions on a weekly
—and sometimes daily—basis.

But, as Emerson had pointed out, smugglers
didn't leave records behind, and I'd just have to let
it go. The important thing was that I was having
that damn hole repaired...and repaired correctly
this time.

After I got back to the shop, I could tell I
hadn't missed much, since Sage was surreptitiously
checking her phone while keeping a single eye on
the front of the store, where one lone shopper—a
woman around my mother's age—was carefully
reading the label on the back of a bottle of arthritis
elixir.

"How'd it go?" Sage asked as she quickly
slipped the phone into a pocket of her dress.

"Just fine," I replied, trying not to smile. I
really didn't care whether she looked at her phone,
as long as doing so didn't prevent her from helping
customers as needed. "I'm going to head downstairs and see how Stu is doing."

She gave me a thumbs-up, and I made my way
to the basement, where more than half of the hole
had already been filled in.

"You're making great progress," I commented,
and Stu gave an unconcerned hitch of his
shoulders.

"Wasn't that big a job," he replied. "Should
have it done by lunch."

"Thank you," I said, and meant it. The sooner that hole was closed up, the better. It didn't look as if we'd had any incursions by rats or other subterranean critters during the time it had been open, but still, no one liked to have a gaping hole in their basement.

Except, apparently, Tonya Willis. Not that it had been her basement, of course.

I went back upstairs, rang up the sale for the woman with the bottle of arthritis elixir, and did my best to settle into the rest of my day. As promised, Stu finished a little before noon, told me he'd be in touch when he had the bill figured out, and then left.

"So, no more hole?" Sage asked.

"No more hole," I replied. "And thank God for that."

That night I'd be on my own, because Noah said he had some paperwork to deal with that he'd been putting off. While I missed him, it was okay to be alone in the house—or at least, as alone as I could be with a couple of familiars knocking around the place. We ate leftovers, watched TV, and retired to bed at the unheard-of hour of nine-thirty.

And that was just fine. Sometimes it was good to have a quiet night in so I could catch up on my sleep.

I did fall asleep quickly, and slumbered

soundly for a while. If I dreamed, I didn't remember any of bits and pieces of those dreams, until....

It didn't really feel like a dream. No, it felt more like a memory, something that was working hard to dredge itself up from the depths of my subconscious.

I was sitting in a chair—blue velvet, very comfortable and squishy, although I didn't feel particularly comfortable right then. Some kind of invisible bonds held me in that chair, preventing my escape.

And standing in front of me was a half-circle of witches whose faces were mostly unfamiliar to me, ranging from one who had to be in her late sixties or early seventies all the way down to a blonde girl who didn't look any older than Sage.

"What were you doing in our tunnels?" the oldest witch demanded, and with that one question, it all snapped back into place with an almost physical jolt.

Exploring the tunnels...crossing over into Marblehead, although that hadn't been my intention. Getting captured and questioned, and then having the young blonde witch cast some kind of forgetting spell so I wouldn't remember anything of what had happened.

I sat up in bed, fingers clutched in the sheets that covered me. Down near my feet, Milo stirred and looked in my direction, his eyes gleaming in the darkness.

"Is something the matter?"

"No," I said hastily. "Just a bad dream. Go back to sleep."

His head tilted, as if he'd picked up an edge of worry in my tone, but then he curled back up and closed his eyes. I lowered myself down onto my pillow, even as my thoughts raced.

Why would those Marblehead witches have cared whether or not I was in their territory? It wasn't as though such a thing was forbidden. Plenty of Salem witches went to Marblehead—or vice versa—on an almost daily basis. Tonya, for example, had just as many real estate listings there as she did here in Salem.

Tonya Willis. The woman who'd cajoled Emerson into keeping the hole in his basement open. For what purpose, though? So she'd be able to easily come and go without anyone wondering what she was up to?

She was already able to do that because of her real estate business, the practical side of my brain argued. However, most of that business was conducted during regular hours, in public. If she was up to something nefarious, it wouldn't be very easy to hide—real estate professionals tended to live fairly public lives.

This is ridiculous, I thought. *Why in the world*

*would you suspect Tonya of anything? She's been part
of your life since almost the day you were born.*

True...but just because you thought you knew
someone well didn't mean you actually did.

The words she'd said to Detective Finley rang
in my ears.

I was born in Marblehead.

Born there, and lived there for most of her early
life, until her mother—for whatever reason—had
decided to move to Salem. This wasn't too strange,
because my town had more than its share of
witches who'd relocated here because the ability to
be open...to an extent...about their witchiness was
very appealing.

But what if Tonya had never really given up her
allegiance to Marblehead? What if she was still part
of a coven there, in addition to being a member of
our coven here in Salem?

I wanted to think I was reaching with all these
theories. After all, I had no concrete evidence to go
on, nothing except a bunch of little feelings that
added up to the overwhelming worry that Tonya
Willis wasn't who she said she was.

True, she hadn't been in my dream, which I
now guessed wasn't a dream at all, but a suppressed
memory finally swimming up out of my subconscious mind. Why the spell had failed, I wasn't sure,
except that enchantments involving memories
could often be tricky, and weren't something a lot

of witches could even manage. That was probably why the blonde girl's coven had had her cast the spell, even though she was clearly the youngest of the group.

No one else there had possessed the inborn talent to do such a thing.

As for why Tonya hadn't been there, well, I could see why she wouldn't want to take the chance of the memory spell slipping and having me remember that she'd been present. Right now, she had plenty of plausible deniability.

Oodles of it, since all this was wild speculation on my part. Something kept telling me I was on the right track, though.

And tomorrow, I'd have to do something about it.

But not until after work, because I'd made Sage cover for me enough times already and all I had to go on at the moment was hunches and gut feelings. When I woke up that morning, I'd been more certain than ever that something terrible was going on with Tonya Willis, even if I couldn't quite put a finger on how or why she would behave in such a way.

So, I did my best to act natural at work, and then when the day was blessedly over, I got in my

Discovery and drove, not home, but over to my mother's house.

I hadn't given her any notice that I was coming, so she looked very surprised when she opened the door.

"Charity!" she exclaimed. "Is everything all right?"

"I don't know," I said grimly. "But we need to talk."

Her brows lifted. Luckily, though, she didn't ask any other questions, and only stepped out of the way so I could come inside.

Not much had changed about the house since I moved out almost seven years earlier, although she'd bought a new set of green velvet couches for the living room that looked almost identical to the ones I remembered from my childhood days. We didn't go in there, however, but instead moved on to the kitchen, where the table that overlooked the lush garden—all flowers, unlike mine, which had a mixture of herbs and edible plants in addition to the blooming varieties—had been the setting for most of our important conversations.

After we'd sat down—and after she'd offered me a glass of iced tea, which I gratefully accepted—she said, "What's going on? Is it something about Sela Warren?"

"It could be," I replied. "I honestly don't know how all this is connected, but I feel like it must be."

A frown creased my mother's brows, but she merely said, "Well, I think you need to tell me all about it, then."

I had to admit that it felt kind of wonderful to unburden myself to my mother, to lay out every single little detail I could recall about Sela's disappearance and Anna's death and the hole in my basement, and not have to censor myself the way I did with pretty much anyone else. Oh, I enjoyed being with Noah, more than I could even acknowledge to myself, but at the same time, I always had to watch what I said, always had to make sure I never let anything slip that might lead him to believe there was more going on with me—and a lot of the women of my acquaintance—than I wanted to let on.

Throughout the entire recitation, my mother listened carefully, her frown deepening. She didn't interrupt, though, and that told me more than anything that she understood how much I'd needed to lay out the whole mess to someone else so they could let me know whether I might actually have something here, or whether I was really letting my imagination run away with me this time.

When I was done and had reached for my iced tea to take a much-needed sip, she gave a very small head shake before saying, "I don't want to believe any of this...but I know I can believe you. Also...."

The word sort of drifted off into the ether, as if

continuing with the sentence would have forced her to utter things she hadn't wanted to acknowledge.

"'Also' what?" I prompted.

She drank some of her own tea, clearly using the slight delay to gather her thoughts. "It's just that now that you've laid all this out in front of me, some things are starting to add up."

I tilted my head in question, and she took a breath and continued.

"Small things. Tonya often misses our solstice and equinox gatherings, but I always told myself it was because her work kept her busy and at the mercy of her clients' schedules, rather than the other way around. But it would make sense if she was dividing her time between us and a coven in Marblehead."

"Why the secrecy, though?" I asked, genuinely curious. "I mean, I've never heard of it happening before, but is it really that big a deal if a witch is connected to more than one coven?"

"Not usually," my mother replied, that one worried furrow between her brows never completely disappearing. "It's not as if we swear a blood oath to be loyal to our covens or anything close to that. They're more like...social groups."

"Well, ours is," I said, remembering the stony faces of the witches in the Marblehead coven, the way they'd talked about how I'd invaded their territory. "I get the feeling that some others take it a lot more seriously."

Her mouth twitched ever so slightly. "You're right about that. Back in the day, some covens were nothing to be trifled with. But none of us have operated like that for generations."

"It seems like the Marblehead one does," I replied, then amended, "Well, this particular Marblehead coven. I recognized a couple of the members, but I know they never told me their names, so it seems like they're doing their best to maintain a low profile."

"Understandable, if they're trying to come and go from their town to ours with no one noticing." My mother paused there, her fingers tight around the tall glass that sat on the table in front of her. "And especially if they're guilty of anything close to what you think they are."

"It makes sense, doesn't it?" I said. "An awful kind of sense, but still. I hate to believe that Tonya Willis could be guilty of blackmail and murder, but...."

"But the signs seem to be pointing there," my mother finished for me, her voice heavy. "I hate to believe it, too—Tonya's been a part of our coven since she came here when she was only fifteen years old. I was in my early twenties back then, but I still wanted her to be my friend and know that she would be accepted here."

"Did her mother ever say why they moved to Salem?" I asked, feeling as though the reason for their relocation might be one of the missing pieces to the puzzle. "I mean, I know witches sometimes do that, but parents usually try to avoid uprooting their kids during high school if possible."

"Iris never really said," my mother replied. "That is, everyone assumed it was because she bought a restaurant here in town, but no one truly knew why she'd decided to do that in the first place."

"I didn't know Mrs. Willis was in the restaurant business," I said, and my mother smiled a little.

"Well, she passed away only a year after you were born, so there was no reason for you to know that. And by that point, Tonya was already out of college and getting on with her life. She'd always been ambitious, so none of us were too surprised when she went into real estate. Making money was always important to her."

"For its own sake, or because of the power it would give her?"

For a moment, my mother was silent, considering my question. Then she said, "I don't really know."

∾

These developments were obviously too massive for us to keep to ourselves, so my mother and I decided we needed to talk to Grace Bowersby next. Soon enough, we'd have to gather the entire coven —well, sans Tonya Willis, for obvious reasons— but right now, we wanted to get a read on Grace's thoughts to see if she agreed that we needed to question Tonya, or whether we'd both gone bonkers.

But Grace listened to everything we had to say and gave a solemn nod. "I'd also often wondered why Tonya missed so many of our meetings over the years," she said. "And while it's not common, sometimes witches do split their loyalties between covens. As for everything else...Anna's death and the rest of this whole mess...we really need to hear Tonya's side of things. We can't convict her without giving her a chance to speak her piece."

"How are we supposed to do that?" I asked. We were all sitting in Grace's comfortable, overstuffed living room, although my mother and I had both declined her offer of tea, since we'd just consumed several iced teas at my mother's house. "It's not as if we can put her on trial."

Grace and my mother shared a weighted glance.

"Actually, we can," my mother said. "Or at least, we can have the witch version of a trial. We can call a coven meeting and set up spells that affect Tonya's magic—and only Tonya's magic. We can also cast a spell that compels her to tell the truth. It's safer than trying to get her to drink a truth potion, since there's no guarantee she'd accept the offer of a drink if we made one."

I thought of how I'd gotten Trevor Miller's mother to drink a truth potion I'd concocted and had to agree. Luckily, Lorna Miller hadn't balked at taking a sip of the iced tea she'd brought for both of us, but if she hadn't, I would have been in a world of hurt.

"Well, Izzy will have to do the truth spell," Grace commented, naming Sage's mother. "None of the rest of us were ever very good at that particular enchantment."

"Still," my mother said. "We should be able to take care of it without too much trouble."

She sounded very blithe, while I was experiencing more and more doubts.

What if I was horribly wrong about all this? What if there was a perfectly logical explanation for Tonya's behavior? We would be accusing her of the worst of crimes with absolutely no evidence.

She would never forgive any of us. Or at least, while she might someday find it within herself to forgive my mother and Grace and the other members of the coven, who were only acting on the information I'd given them, I kind of doubted she'd ever want to have any further interactions with me.

Well, except to maybe spit in my face when she bumped into me at Market Basket.

Possibly sensing some of the uncertainty roiling in me, Grace leaned over and put a reassuring hand on my arm. "Your instincts were proven right in the last two murder cases you had to deal with," she said quietly. "There is no reason to believe you aren't right about this. As you told us, there are lots of strange pieces that don't really fit together... unless Tonya is the glue."

"And the sooner we find out, the better," my mother declared.

Another thought struck me. "What if Tonya doesn't even show up?" I asked. "After all, she's already proved that she doesn't seem to care much about attending our meetings."

"Oh, she'll be there," Grace replied, sounding uncharacteristically grim.

"We'll make sure of it."

Chapter 17

Gland Illusion

WE HAD THE MEETING AT IZZY'S HOUSE, mostly because it felt like more neutral ground, and also because her participation was a necessity if we were going to get Tonya to tell the truth about her involvement—if any—in the death of Anna Warren and Sela's strange flight to Rome.

Unlike my mother's and Grace's houses, Izzy's place didn't have a real basement, so the meeting was held in her living room. Like Izzy herself, it had a slightly bohemian, disheveled feel that was still charming in a way you couldn't quite quantify. I thought she could give Sela Warren a run for her money when it came to having plants everywhere, since philodendrons and string-of-pearl plants cascaded from the overstuffed bookshelves, and various types of ficus in varying heights and shapes crowded every corner.

I was a little surprised to see Sage there, since she rarely attended impromptu meetings like this one. However, her mother had probably impressed on her that it was very important to be here and that she definitely shouldn't sit this one out.

Even more startling was the presence of Elise Figg, who looked ill at ease but also determined, as if she wanted to be here to hear for herself who her blackmailer had been. Clearly, either my mother or Grace—or maybe both of them—had decided it was important for there to be a quorum so we'd be at our greatest possible strength, even if one of those attending had been formally shunned.

In fact, the only coven member I didn't see was Stella Monroe, but since she was nursing a newborn baby, her absence could probably be forgiven.

Tonya wasn't here yet—on purpose, since she'd been given an arrival time fifteen minutes later than the rest of us so there wouldn't be any risk that anyone would be missing when she showed up— and so we'd have enough time to cast the spells to contain her magic before she arrived. Everyone looked a little ill at ease, which wasn't too surprising, considering the reason why we were all here.

Tonya Willis, powers confined,

In our aura, your magic's bind,
No harm or hex shall ever prevail,
Within this ward, your spells shall fail.

We'd hardly finished uttering the last words of the spell before the doorbell rang. Looking flustered, Izzy hurried over to answer it.

"Oh, hi, Tonya," she said, the words coming out in almost a gasp. The world's best actress, she definitely wasn't. "So glad you could make it."

Tonya entered the living room and sent a smile at all of us that was anything but genuine. In contrast to the casual and/or boho outfits the rest of us had on, she wore a slim skirt and a sleeveless silk blouse, and looked as though she'd just come from a house showing.

"No problem," she replied, although the edge to her voice told me she'd guessed it actually was a problem, even if she didn't yet know the full extent of it. "I'm just glad I don't have any more house showings today. What's the reason for this gathering?"

Looking somewhat like a mouse deciding to take on a swooping hawk, Izzy planted herself in front of Tonya and chanted,

Tonya Willis, speak no lies,
Truth be told, as the spell complies.

At once, Tonya's sharp eyes went glassy, just like Lorna Miller's had when I'd dosed her with a truth potion. However, Tonya appeared even more out of it, and seemed to sway where she stood, like a slender tree caught in a brisk breeze.

Valerie Monroe stepped forward. She was the oldest of us, and the one Tonya looked on the most as an authority figure, which was exactly why we'd asked her to open the questioning.

"Tonya Willis, are you a member of a coven in Marblehead?"

"Yes," she said in dreamy tones, then added, "It's my coven. I run it."

All of us Salem witches exchanged a glance. We didn't have anything like a head of our coven, and we shared responsibilities equally based on whoever's abilities seemed most suited to a certain magical task. True, we tended to defer to Valerie, but that was only because of her age and wisdom.

"How long have you run this coven?" Valerie asked next.

"Since my mother died," Tonya responded. "That's how it's always worked—our coven has passed from mother to daughter since the days when Marblehead was first settled."

That answer surprised me, just because I couldn't understand why Tonya and her mother had come to Salem when they had a heritage so firmly embedded in the neighboring town.

Valerie must have been thinking much the same thing, because she inquired, "If your roots go so deep in Marblehead, then why come to Salem?"

"My mother hoped she could take over the coven here as well," Tonya said, her placid-sounding voice a direct contrast to the chilling content of her words. "You looked weak from the outside. But once she was here and had insinuated herself into your coven, she realized you were strong...as were the other covens here in Salem. She thought about going back to Marblehead but decided people would ask too many questions. So, we stayed."

Well, I supposed I should feel somewhat gratified that Tonya and her mother had learned we Salem witches weren't a bunch of pushovers.

"But you remained active in the Marblehead coven at the same time," Valerie said, and Tonya nodded.

"Of course," she said calmly. "That was my coven. I controlled it after my mother died."

"Controlled it how?" I interjected, knowing the words had come out way too sharp.

Izzy sent me a warning glance, as if to let me know I needed to moderate my tone in case I disrupted her spell. I hadn't known it was that fragile, and prayed I hadn't made Tonya snap right out of it.

To my infinite relief, she still looked dreamy

and nothing like her usual brisk self. Head tilted slightly to one side, she responded, "We needed the strongest, best coven possible. That was why the women of my line told the witches in their coven who they could breed with, so we wouldn't have any weaklings among us."

The look of horror on my face was echoed on the faces of the other women in my coven. Voice somehow steady, my mother said, "You had a breeding program?"

"If you want to call it that," Tonya said. "That's why I was so angry with Sela Warren. She wanted to marry that doctor even though I told her she couldn't be with him, that because her mother had died of cancer, there was too much chance of her passing those genetic markers on to her children, and so she needed to live her life alone, like her sister Anna. That happens sometimes...we Willis witches have to snip off a line because of health issues that pop up."

Even though Izzy's living room was warm enough—downright stuffy, if I wanted to be honest about it—every inch of my body felt as though it had just been dropped into the mid-Atlantic in January.

Now I understood why Sela had fled the country with the man she loved, had tried so hard to keep her true destination a secret from everyone.

"But why kill Anna?" Valerie Monroe asked, her voice harder and colder than I'd ever heard it, like the icy north where her granddaughter's husband, the frost-elf Kai, had been born.

"Oh, that was an accident," Tonya said airily. "I set the death spell on Sela's house, thinking it would catch her as soon as she walked in the door. But she'd already run away somewhere, and Anna went to the house instead, for whatever reason... probably to water the plants, I'm assuming. Spells like that don't discriminate, you know. It was set to catch the first witch who entered the property—which should have been Sela—and so it caught Anna."

An accident. Well, I supposed that was one way of looking at it...except there was nothing accidental about the kind of horrible enchantment Tonya Willis had set on Sela Warren's house.

"And you were angry with Sela, so you blackmailed me into putting a hex on her familiar, hoping that would dissuade her from being with Colin Novak," Elise put in. Her tone was so flat that I knew she had to be expending all kinds of energy to keep herself from screaming at the other witch in rage and betrayal.

"That was my original plan, yes," Tonya replied. "I couldn't do it myself, because my magic is sometimes too strong, and I needed a spell that would be a nuisance but wouldn't actually hurt her familiar. But Sela was tougher than I thought she would be. She gave the hedgehog to Charity to watch, then ran away with her doctor boyfriend."

She sounded utterly unconcerned about the whole thing, as though it was no big deal that the hex might have caused me some actual injury, rather than a few near-misses. Across the room, Elise watched the other woman with narrow eyes, her compressed, pale lips telling me exactly how she felt about being used to further such an evil woman's ends.

"And the tunnel?" I pressed, since I'd been wondering about that all along. "Were you using it to go back and forth between Salem and Marblehead without being detected?"

Tonya nodded. "Yes, it was very useful...for a time. But then Emerson said he was selling the store, and I knew if I pressed him too hard on the subject, he'd become suspicious and start asking too many questions. So I let it go, and instead made sure to have plenty of house listings in Marblehead so no one would wonder why I was going over there so often."

It sounded to me as though she'd done her best to cover all the bases. I wondered, when she'd lied about so many other things, why she hadn't told me Anna Warren's death had been due to natural causes, since I hadn't been able to detect any dark magic around her. However, I guessed she'd decided it was better to be truthful in that one time, just in case any other witches detected the spell that had killed Anna and mentioned the discrepancy.

"I've heard enough," my mother announced then, echoing a sentiment we probably all shared. Tonya had admitted her guilt in both Anna's death and Elise's blackmailing, so at this point, we really needed to figure out how in the world we were going to proceed.

"She's definitely guilty beyond all shadow of a doubt," Valerie agreed. "The problem is...what do we do now? It's not as if we can turn her in to the police."

In detached tones, Tonya said, "If a witch in my coven did anything like this, we would put her to death."

She sounded as if she was talking about someone else's fate other than her own, but I guessed that was just Izzy's truth spell being a little too effective.

"We have to destroy her magic," Elise said, and we all stared at her in surprise.

"There's no way to do anything like that," I protested. "Our magic is born in us."

Elise only tilted her head slightly, her expression now almost amused. "True, it's born in us—but only because it's physically part of our natures. A mutation in the pineal gland."

I blinked at her, and my mother and Valerie and Sage all looked startled as well. Clearly, this was the first time any of them had heard anything about this.

But I noticed how Grace's gaze dropped to the floor, and she appeared more worried than surprised by Elise's announcement.

"You knew about this supposed mutation?" I demanded.

Grace gave an embarrassed little shrug. "Well, you know I take witch history very seriously. That includes some of the less...savory...aspects of our community."

"What she's trying to say," Elise put in, "is that back in the middle of the nineteenth century, a witch named Tabitha Beckett got permission from the other members of her coven to perform autopsies on the bodies of local witches who had recently passed away. I'm assuming she also did autopsies on mundanes to get a control group, although it was never explicitly explained. Anyway, she discovered that witches have a certain mutation in their pineal glands that allows them to perform magic. She could never completely explain the mechanism involved, but the mutation—which is genetic—is what gives us our magic. All I have to do is focus on Tonya's pineal gland and destroy it, and she won't ever be able to practice magic again."

We all stared at Elise, clearly flabbergasted by this development.

"Can a person live without a pineal gland?" Sage asked, the first time she'd spoken so far. It seemed pretty clear to me that she'd preferred to let her elders handle this messy matter, but curiosity had prompted her to speak at last.

"Sure," Elise said easily. "She may end up with some sleep disorders, because the pineal gland helps to regulate our circadian rhythms, but medication can help her with that." Voice hardening, she added, "Compared to what she's done, I think she'd be getting off pretty lightly."

I couldn't argue with that observation...and apparently no one else could, either, because an uneasy silence fell.

"Any other objections?" Elise asked then, her tone turning wry.

"No—no," Valerie replied. "I think I speak for all of us when I say that this seems like the best solution to a very messy problem."

Elise's mouth curled slightly. "That's what I thought."

She turned toward Tonya, who'd stood there silently during all this, not seeming very concerned about her fate. Now Elise's expression turned blank, as if she was doing her best to control her anger and instead channel it into the spell she was about to cast.

When she spoke, her tone was cool, almost indifferent...although the words of the spell were anything but that.

By moon's decree and starlight's grace,
    I strip your power from this place.
    Witch's magic, now undone,
    In darkness, you'll be left with none.

When Elise was finished, Tonya continued to stand there motionless, her eyes as wide and glassy and emotionless as a doll's.

"She'll probably be out of it for a while," Elise commented. "One of us should drive her home and put her to bed."

"I'll do it," my mother offered. "Once I have her settled, I can just walk home."

This seemed like the best solution, since my mother only lived two doors down from Tonya, and there wouldn't be any of the messiness involved in needing to have someone else follow along and provide a ride home afterward. As to how we'd deal with her on a daily basis going forward, well, I supposed we'd just have to figure that out. This was definitely an unprecedented situation.

A sudden thought occurred to me. "What'll happen when Tonya's coven finds out she no longer has magical powers?"

Grace frowned. "It's hard to say," she replied. "It could be that someone else takes over, or—"

"Or they'll fall apart quickly enough, which is what often happens when a dictatorship collapses," my mother said crisply. "We'll keep an eye on them, but I have a feeling the witches of Tonya's coven will be very glad she won't be making decisions for them anymore."

I hoped she was right.

As with so many other things, only time would tell.

Going home after the coven meeting felt like something of an anticlimax, but there wasn't anything else I could really do. I needed to check on the familiars, and Noah and I had been discussing possibly going out. However, the last thing I wanted right now was to see him...not because I didn't enjoy being in his company, but because I feared he'd take one look at my face and immediately know something massive had happened earlier today.

Maybe at some point, I'd decide he truly was "the one" and that I could be completely open with him, but that day wasn't today.

Instead, I texted him to say I was feeling tired and that I just wanted to plop down on the couch and chill, adding,

Rain check?

Sure. Hopefully, you'll feel better tomorrow. Maybe we can go out to eat somewhere.

I hoped I would be feeling better, too. Surely twenty-four hours or so would help to cushion the blow of all the terrible things I'd heard today.

Fingers crossed.

Sounds like a plan. Have a great evening.

You, too.

All right, I'd made sure I would have a quiet evening at home. Now I just had to decide what to do with it.

I was standing in front of the refrigerator, wondering if I had the energy to actually cook something or whether I should just cave and get DoorDash, when the doorbell rang.

At once, I frowned. I didn't get many visitors, I knew Noah wasn't coming over, and it was definitely the wrong time of year to get a call from Girl Scouts selling cookies or high school kids trying to get me to buy candy to support their latest fundraiser.

Well, only one way to find out.

I opened the door and felt my mouth drop open in shock.

Sela Warren stood there, looking tanned and glowing and utterly unlike the nervous, frightened woman who'd dropped off her familiar two weeks ago.

"You heard?" I blurted, and she sent me a confused look.

"Heard about what?"

This was definitely a conversation we shouldn't be having on the front porch. "Come on in," I said, and stepped out of the way so she could enter the house. As soon as we got to the living room, her gaze moved around the space, obviously looking for Lionel. "Lionel's outside," I told her quickly so she wouldn't have to worry. "He and Milo like being in the garden at this time of day. And he's doing great —the hex was lifted, so he's just been enjoying his time here."

Sela blinked. Besides looking bronzed and relaxed, she also had a wide gold band on the fourth finger of her left hand, further evidence that her Roman holiday had gone very well for her. "That's—that's great news," she replied, then hesitated. "And I'm really sorry about the hex. I honestly thought Tonya had cast it on me, and as soon as I left Lionel with you and I was out of the country, we'd all be safe." Another pause before she went on, "Was everything okay?"

Since I'd escaped mostly unscathed and the warranty would cover my TV's replacement, I said, "Everything was fine. We were able to figure it out and get it taken care of before anything got too bad."

Sela nodded, obviously relieved by this news. Then she asked, "But what did you mean about me 'hearing' something?"

"About Tonya," I said. She blinked in confusion, and I went on, "Maybe you should sit down. Would you like something to drink?"

"A glass of water would be great," she said. "We got into JFK earlier today, and Colin went on to Marblehead while I came here to get Lionel, but I'm still feeling kind of dehydrated from the plane ride."

I told her that was no problem, then hurried into the kitchen so I could grab a glass from the cupboard and pour some water into it from the pitcher I kept in the fridge. When I got back, I handed over the glass, and she took a large swallow.

"Okay," she said, and her expression darkened slightly, as if she wasn't sure she wanted to hear what I had to say, but knew she needed to press on. "What's this about Tonya?"

"We found out what she did," I replied. "To your sister, to your coven. I'm very sorry."

Sela's mouth tightened, and I could tell from the way she blinked that she was trying her hardest not to cry. "You found out," she said, her voice shaking slightly. "Did you do anything about it?"

I wanted to retort that Tonya should have been her own coven's problem, not ours, but I reminded myself that Sela must be in a lot of pain over the loss of her sister, and I needed to be gentle. "We did," I said. "One of our coven members burned out her ability to use magic. She'll never be able to control you—or anyone else—ever again."

For a long moment, Sela sat there in silence, obviously trying to absorb this information, to understand that Tonya was no longer a threat to her, or to her happiness. Quietly, she said, "Thank you."

"I'm just glad we were able to do something," I replied. "But I have to ask—if you didn't know that Tonya had been taken out of commission, why did you show up now?"

Now Sela smiled, her sorrow of a moment before, if not exactly erased, a little softened. "Because I'm pregnant," she said simply. "That's why I told you I had to stay away a while longer. I had to know for sure before I came back. Once I was carrying Colin's child, there wasn't anything Tonya could do to me."

I hated to ask, but considering all the evil Tonya Willis had perpetrated in her lifetime, I had to know. "She wouldn't...try to stop you from having the child?"

Sela shook her head. "There were lengths to which even she wouldn't go. Also, another child born to the coven would still be valuable, even if that child's father wasn't the one she would have chosen for me. I'd had my suspicions before Colin and I even left for Rome, but I wasn't positive until yesterday when I went to see a doctor there."

"Well...congratulations," I said, since I wasn't sure how else I could respond.

"Thank you. Colin's deliriously happy—he always wanted a family, but his ex-wife kept putting it off until he realized she would never have kids. Which is her choice, but it's not what he wanted."

And now he had a new wife and a baby on the way, and no worries about their future.

Except....

"What do you think your coven will do now?" I asked, echoing my question to my mother earlier today.

"They'll fall apart," Sela replied at once, her tone firm enough that it didn't seem as if there were any doubts in her mind on that particular subject. "Without Tonya controlling everything, they won't know what to do with themselves. They might try to form a new coven, but I have a feeling most of them will just go it alone for a while, or maybe try to see if one of the other Marblehead covens will have them." She shrugged, obviously not too worried about the fate of her other coven members. "But I'm fine just concentrating on my family...and saying goodbye to my sister." A little pause, and she added, "I think we'll name the baby Anna."

Because of course she would have a daughter. That was just what witches did.

And being named after Sela's late sister was a fitting tribute to the aunt the little girl would never know.

I hoped she would grow up to be as tough and resourceful as her mother.

Sela took Lionel home after that, and Milo and I stood on the porch and waved goodbye as they drove away.

"Do you ever get over it?" he inquired.

"Over what?" I said, although I thought I knew what he was asking.

"Saying goodbye."

I bent down and patted him on the head. "I don't know if it's a question of getting 'over it,'" I commented. "I think it's more knowing that I've done my best to help a familiar, and now they can go back to their regular lives and help their mistresses again. It's important work."

Milo gave a solemn nod. "I suppose I can see

that. Still...I'm sad. We had Cinny and then Lionel one after the other, and now it's just the two of us again."

"Not forever," I said. "Another familiar will come along. And besides, it may be just the two of us tonight, but I'll be seeing Noah tomorrow, and I'm pretty sure I can convince him to bring you with us to Mercy Tavern or someplace else where we can eat on the patio."

It wouldn't even take that much convincing. Noah loved Milo and would be all too happy to have him join us for dinner.

Maybe we weren't quite a family...not yet...but I thought we were well on our way there.

A few days later, I was startled to see Emerson come into the shop. As far as I could remember, he'd never visited after the property changed hands, and I'd just figured he hadn't thought it necessary to see what I'd done with my store, and didn't have any need of arthritis elixirs or tinctures to help with insomnia.

He glanced around at our surroundings, his expression pleased. I had to admit that the shop was looking pretty good right then, since Sela and Maggie had come by just the day before with the plants I'd ordered, and had arranged them in tasteful locations around the store.

"It's very nice," he said after I'd greeted him. We were alone in the shop, because Sage had run out to get some iced tea, and I was experiencing a rare Friday-afternoon lull. "I suppose I should have stopped by before now."

"Well, I can see how it might have felt strange to have the place look so different from the way it was when you owned it," I replied. "Is there something in particular I can help you with?"

His gaze moved across the rows of bottles on the shelf behind me as if he was studying their labels, and then he shook his head. "No, not really. I just wanted to come in and thank you."

"Thank me?" I said blankly, not sure what he meant.

"For our little conversation the other day," he explained. "I was thinking about Aria, about how Tonya had always been so firm about not wanting me to be a part of my daughter's life. Well, it might have been twenty-five years too late, but I went ahead and reached out to Aria, and told her the truth...and that I understood if she didn't want to have anything to do with me."

Approaching his long-lost daughter like that had taken some guts. Of course, now he didn't have to fear any magical retaliation on Tonya's part for what she would probably view as meddling, but he didn't know that.

And with Tonya forever altered by what the coven had done to her, it was probably good that Aria would have her newfound father to lean on from now on.

"What happened?" I asked.

Emerson smiled. "She cried, and then she told me she'd always wanted to know who I was. Said she was proud to know I was her father, and that she hoped to see me in the audience at her next concert."

Warm tears pricked at my eyes. Aria and I had never been close, because I was just enough older that we hadn't shared any classes in school, but still, I'd liked her and always wanted the best for her. "That's wonderful to hear."

"Yes," he said simply. "I'll just have to do what I can to make up for lost time. You have a good day, Ms. Hughes."

He inclined his head toward me and then went out, tall and elegant among the shorts-clad shoppers that crowded the sidewalks of Essex Street.

I watched him go, then reached up to blot away the tears that still stung my eyes. Yes, Tonya Willis had done a lot of harm in her life, but the pain she'd inflicted on those around her was already beginning to heal. Soon enough, she'd fade into obscurity, her powers gone...and with them, the ability to cause any more damage.

It might not have been the ending I was expecting when all this began, but I'd take it.

I'd definitely take it.

The End

~

Charity's adventures will continue in *Charms and Chihuahuas,* releasing in March 2024.

Also by Christine Pope

Cauldrons and Cats

Hexes and Hedgehogs

Charms and Chihuahuas (April 2024)

LATTES AND LEVITATION

(Cozy Mystery/Paranormal Romance)

Caffeine Before Curses

Muffins After Magic

Pastries and Prophecies

Eclairs and Ectoplasm

Sugar Skulls and Specters

Wedding Cakes and Wishes

HEDGEWITCH FOR HIRE

(Cozy Mystery/Paranormal Romance)

Grave Mistake

Social Medium

Household Demons

Perpetual Potion

Jingle Spells

Wandering Monsters

Uninvited Ghosts

Prophet Motive

Ballroom Bits

Spell Check

Brew Confessions (February 2024)

UNEXPECTED MAGIC*

(Urban Fantasy/Paranormal Romance)

Found Objects

Finders, Keepers

Lost and Found

Finding Destiny

THE WITCHES OF WHEELER PARK*

(Paranormal Romance)

Storm Born

Thunder Road

Winds of Change

Mind Games

A Wheeler Park Christmas

Blood Ties

Healing Hands

Wishful Thinking

Smoke and Mirrors

MISS PRIMM'S ACADEMY FOR WAYWARD WITCHES*

(Fantasy/Academy Romance)

Misspelled

Dispelled

Expelled

PROJECT DEMON HUNTERS*

(Paranormal Romance)

Unquiet Souls

Unbound Spirits

Unholy Ground

Unseen Voices

Unmarked Graves

Unbroken Vows

THE DEVIL YOU KNOW*

(Paranormal Romance)

Sympathy for the Devil

Charmed, I'm Sure

A Wing and a Prayer

Wish Upon a Star

THE WITCHES OF CANYON ROAD*

(Paranormal Romance)

Hidden Gifts

Darker Paths

Mysterious Ways

A Canyon Road Christmas

Demon Born

An Ill Wind

Higher Ground

Haunted Hearts

THE WITCHES OF CLEOPATRA HILL*

(Paranormal Romance)

Darkangel

Darknight

Darkmoon

Sympathetic Magic

Protector

Spellbound

A Cleopatra Hill Christmas

Impractical Magic

Strange Magic

The Arrangement

Defender

Bad Blood

Deep Magic

Darktide

(Paranormal/Science Fiction Romance)

Bad Vibrations

Desert Hearts

Angel Fire

Star Crossed

Falling Angels

Enemy Mine

TALES OF THE LATTER KINGDOMS*

(Fantasy Romance)

All Fall Down

Dragon Rose

Binding Spell

Ashes of Roses

One Thousand Nights

Threads of Gold

The Wolf of Harrow Hall

Moon Dance

The Song of the Thrush

THE GAIAN CONSORTIUM SERIES*

(Science Fiction Romance)

Beast (free prequel novella)

Blood Will Tell

Breath of Life

The Gaia Gambit

The Mandala Maneuver

The Titan Trap

The Zhore Deception

The Refugee Ruse

STANDALONE TITLES

Hearts on Fire (Paranormal Romance)

Taking Dictation (Contemporary Romance)

Golden Heart (Gaslight Fantasy Romance)

Night Music: A Modern Reimagining of The Phantom
of the Opera (Contemporary Romance)

Ghost Dance: A Sequel to Gaston Leroux's The
Phantom of the Opera (Historical Mystery/Romance)

Flight Before Christmas (Fantasy Romance)

* Indicates a completed series

About the Author

USA Today bestselling author Christine Pope has been writing stories ever since she commandeered her family's Smith-Corona typewriter back in grade school. Her work includes paranormal romance, cozy paranormal mystery, and urban fantasy, among others. She makes her home in New Mexico.

Christine Pope on the Web:
www.christinepope.com

 facebook.com/ChristinePopeAuthor
bookbub.com/authors/christine-pope
youtube.com/@ChristinePopeAuthor